WAVE OF THE FUTURE

Jefferson followed Garvey out into the corridor. Seeing that they were alone, he said, "Let's have it."

"A question first. What do you know about cloning?"

"It is something that doesn't concern me greatly because it is a scientific matter, not a military one."

"Except you have a platoon that has been cloned."

"Certainly," said Jefferson. "An experimental unit that is temporarily attached to my command."

Garvey stepped closer and lowered his voice. "The techniques for cloning humans were developed ten years ago."

"So what?" Then Jefferson's face went white. He shook himself and said, "But they all look to be twenty, twenty-one years old."

"That's what threw me, too. But I asked the doctor about accelerating the growth of certain plants and then animals. What we're seeing is the wave of the future."

"Soldiers, humans designed to be soldiers, grown quickly through childhood and suddenly thrown out into the world." He stared at Garvey. "How old are they? Really?"

"The information suggests, based on what I've seen in the last—"

"How old?" demanded Jefferson.

"Seven."

"Are you sure?"

"Positive."

"Good God."

Ace Books by Kevin Randle

Jefferson's War Series

THE GALACTIC SILVER STAR
THE PRICE OF COMMAND
THE LOST COLONY
THE JANUARY PLATOON

DEATH OF A REGIMENT
(coming in November)

JEFFERSON'S WAR
THE JANUARY PLATOON
KEVIN RANDLE

ACE BOOKS, NEW YORK

1

RECRUITMENT AND TRAINING CENTER, OLD EARTH

JOHN, SIX ONE TWO, Smith was older than his brothers and sisters by a matter of minutes and that was why he sat in the lone chair at the front of the training center. To his left, two feet behind him, sat Sara, Six One Three, Smith, senior to all the other brothers and sisters because of a quirk in the order in which things had been accomplished. Arrayed behind them were the remaining forty brothers and sisters, the oldest ones taking the positions of squad leader and the next oldest as the assistant squad leaders, the rest broken down into fire team leaders and fire teams based solely on age.

John, Six One Two, Smith was a tall, slender man who looked to be twenty-one years old. He had pale skin, from lack of time in the sun, black hair that looked darker than it was because of his white skin, blue eyes, and sharp features. There were no marks on his skin anywhere. There were no childhood scars, or wrinkles, or blemishes. If his was a hide taken by a hunter, it would have been considered A1 prime.

Sara, Six One Three, Smith was a tall, slender woman who looked to be twenty-one years old. Her black hair was longer than her brother's, cut in what had once been called a pageboy. Her eyes were blue and her features sharp. If you had stood John, Six One Two, next to his sister, Sara, Six One Three, you would have sworn they were identical twins, except that one was male and the other was female. It was a puzzle created by those who understood genetics and gene-splicing and cloning and test-tube creations.

The remainder of the brothers and sisters were the mirror images of John, Six One Two, and Sara, Six One Three. They were as interchangeable as the peas in a pod or the grains of sand on a beach. One looked like the next who looked like the next. The only difference was in their ages which was determined by a random draw.

John, Six One Two, sat wrapped in a plush chair that nearly engulfed him. There was a small band around his head, feeding into contacts placed against his skull. At the moment, he was learning how to set fields of fire when creating a base camp for a small unit. In his mind, he could see a platoon-sized unit, equipped with the weapons of the late twentieth century, as they placed the squad automatic weapons, the grenadiers, and finally the riflemen, to make the best use of the terrain and for the protection of the camp. Once he understood the concept, it made perfect sense to him.

Sara, Six One Three, sat in a similar chair with a similar headband, and she too was learning to set fields of fire, but from the point of view of a well-trained, knowledgeable NCO and not that of a young officer with his first command in the field.

And behind, the brothers and sisters were learning similar tasks in a similar fashion whether it was the placement of a single machine gun or the duties of a rifleman on the line.

Finished with the review, John, Six One Two, stripped the headband and hooked it over the top of the chair. He then glanced up at the stage that was wrapped in shadows. A moment later the recessed lights came on and a tall, skinny woman walked to the center of it. She was about thirty, had blonde hair, a long, pointed nose and a pointed chin. If she had tried, she would have been nice-looking, but she didn't try.

She waited until all the headbands had been removed and all eyes were on her. She stood with her hands behind her back, rocking forward and back on her feet, impatient with the lethargic attitude of the younger people in front of her.

"Today is the day," she announced, and then waited for some kind of a reaction. When none of the people in front of her moved or spoke, she added, "We have been going over that which you should already know only because transport to the regiment has not been available."

Again she waited and still there was no reaction. She wasn't sure if they had been that well trained or if they had all had their emotions surgically removed. None of them ever seemed to smile or laugh or cry or get angry. She wasn't sure that they couldn't communicate with one another through telepathy or some other nonverbal skill.

"You are to report to the shuttle pad at zero six thirty with all your field gear, weapons, and personal possessions that you desire to take with you. Questions?" She'd asked for them knowing full well there would be none. There never were.

John, Six One Two, stood up and smoothed down the front of his one-piece, grey coverall. He turned and waited as the remainder of the platoon got to its feet. All were attired as he was. All were the same height. The only differences were the name tapes above the right breast pockets and the rank insignia either on the epaulets or on the sleeves.

"Squad leaders," he said, his voice high. "Take charge of your squads and return to your quarters. Squad leader briefing at seventeen hundred, chow at eighteen thirty and lights out at twenty-two hundred." He didn't ask for questions because there would be none.

As the platoon began to file out of the training center, Sara, Six One Three, stepped closer. "Will there be time for a video tonight?"

"I don't see the point. There is plenty to do without wasting time on entertainment."

She grinned at him, sure that the woman on the stage could not see it. "Sometimes you're a bigger pain in the ass than all the brass hats combined."

"Sometimes you overstep the customs and courtesies."

"You're not that much older," she said.

"No, but I am the commander. You seem to forget that too often."

"And if something happens to you, then I take command," she said softly.

John, Six One Two, glanced at her and knew that she was not making a threat but stating a fact. "When you command, then you command. Until that time, I command."

"Yes, sir," she said and there was no sarcasm in her voice. She understood the situation as well has he did.

Delta Royal Three, as designated on the various navigation charts, was a small, out-of-the-way planet in a small, out-of-the-way system. Its chief attribute was that it had a climate that was remarkably like that of Hawaii on the good days. There was lush vegetation, rich soil, and plentiful rainfall. Transplanted crops, corn, soybeans, and the like grew to huge and delicious fruition. There were no insects or bacteria or weeds that could compete with the Earth seeds. It was a farmer's heaven and because it was off the beaten path, it was nearly undeveloped. Cargo ships landed infrequently but with enough cargo space empty that the crops not used to sustain the colony could be transferred to places that needed them. Not the most efficient way to do things, but one that was working.

Colonist Ralph Moody had opted for Delta Royal Three. He had spent enough time on Earth trying to breathe the golden atmosphere that threatened to choke the healthy and to kill those who had weak lungs. He was tired of standing in line to buy a loaf of bread or to wonder if there would be any meat when the Tuesday allotment was issued. He was tired of being afraid to walk the streets or to let his wife go to the store alone to buy the few things that were offered for sale. He was afraid for his children, knowing there were parasites out there who preyed on the weak and the young and the not-too-bright.

Colony recruiters often worked the lines, telling all who would listen that things were better on the off worlds. There were worlds where the sunlight was bright and the air was clean. There were jobs to be had and for those who didn't want to work for someone else, there were farms that needed tending. Plenty of land was available for those who could get there and take it.

Moody, like the others, listened to the glowing accounts and knew that he could never afford to move his family to an off world. And then he learned that those who moved to the out-of-the-way worlds, the ones that had the clean air and clean water and the healthful environments but that were not on the main shipping routes cost nothing to get to. The government picked up the tab, figuring it was cheaper to move the people off Earth than to have them hanging on welfare or taking handouts or bleeding the system because there was nothing else for them to do. Colonize the outer worlds, get people on them and then begin taxing those people.

Moody discussed it with Martha but not the two kids. It was decided they would ship on the first available craft and not worry about not knowing a thing about farming. How hard could it be? Stick the seeds in the ground, watch them grow, and then harvest the bounty.

And the government did nothing to discourage Moody's simplistic view of farming. They didn't mention crop rotation, soil depletion, insect infestation where the most harmful chemicals were no longer sufficient to deal with the pests, or the lack of rain, or too much rain. They let Moody believe that all he had to do was stick the seeds in the soil and watch them grow.

Except that on Delta Royal Three that was the truth. All Moody had to do was stick the seeds in the ground and watch them grow. No pests to eat them and no weeds that would crowd them out. The soil was so rich and thick that Moody wouldn't have to worry about crop rotation and soil depletion until the middle of the next century. Life was beautiful.

Except for the indigenous local population. They were half human and half brute. Robust creatures about five feet tall with big, hair-covered heads, and brains twice as large as a human's. While they had only the beginnings of a civilization, they were far from stupid. They were bright, imitative creatures that were below the humans on the scale only because the human race was older and had learned more. That didn't imply that the humans were smarter or more civilized, only older.

Moody and his family had landed at the only functioning spaceport, had been met by a representative of the colonial office and driven into the town. There were no paved streets, just mud ruts between buildings that looked to have been scraped together from the mud in the streets and the grasses that grew wild around them. But there were also prefabbed buildings from Earth. They were constructed of a thin, strong material not unlike plastic that was drawn from the elements in the ground around it. A robot and a machine sat on the ground with the machine spitting out the plastic while the robot bent it and massaged it into floors and walls and a roof. When finished, another robot cut doors and windows and erected stairs so they could move to the next floor and do it all again.

Moody was given a vehicle and a map and told to stake out his farm, no more than a hundred hectares to begin, and report back in a week or less. Robots would erect his house and a barn and he would be given seeds. It was up to him to make them grow.

They had settled into the new house with its molded plastic furniture and its video center complete with a library of the latest tapes. It had seemed idyllic.

Until something had uprooted some of his crops. Moody had crouched in the center of the damage and tried to figure out what had done it. There didn't seem to be any gophers or rabbits or anything else around to eat the plants or tear them up. There were no footprints or tracts of any kind. It looked as if the plants had been rejected by the soil.

Martha had walked out after finishing with the breakfast and getting the kids to study by using part of the video library. Some of the tapes were educational in nature.

"What did it?" she asked, crouching near him.

Moody looked at her, thinking that she had adapted to the life quickly. She'd modified the standard coveralls by cutting off the legs to make shorts and then cutting off the sleeves. She didn't bother to fasten the front, leaving it open to the navel so she'd be cool.

"I haven't the faintest," he said.

She picked up a plant and looked at the small ear of corn just beginning to form. "No sign of teeth marks."

"Meaning?"

"That whatever did this wasn't interested in it for food."

Moody nodded and stood up, brushing his hands together. He glanced up at the cloudless morning sky and then turned, looking into the forest, a hundred meters away.

"There are animals on Earth that sometimes uproot plants as a way of making territory."

"I've never heard that."

Moody wiped his hands on the seat of his coveralls. He hadn't let her modify his, though on the hottest days he was sorely tempted and no one had said that the colonists were not allowed to modify the clothes in whatever way the mood moved them.

"What are you going to do?" asked Martha.

Moody shrugged and then said, "I suppose I can ask them in town. This probably isn't the first time something like this happened. They'll tell me how to deal with it."

"Is this going to hurt us?"

Moody glanced at the torn up plants. A quarter hectare was involved, and not all of it had been ripped up. "No," he said. "A nuisance, but nothing more."

There was a rattling in the forest. A rustling that drifted toward them on the light morning breeze. Birds, brightly colored things of red and yellow and orange, launched themselves into the air. They swirled up and away, moving toward the river that was half a klick to the west.

"What's that?" asked Martha.

"Hell, I don't know," said Moody. He took a step forward and watched as four of the natives came crashing out of the forest, running straight at him.

Martha looked at the creatures and then at her husband. On Earth, four men running at her could only be bad news, but it was so quiet and peaceful on Delta Royal Three that she no longer knew what it meant.

The natives were screaming something and Moody thought that it was a warning of some kind. And then he saw the clubs in their hands. Whirling, he screamed, "Run."

But Moody didn't run. He watched as his wife fled, heading toward the house. If she could get in and get the door closed, there was nothing the natives could do to penetrate it short of using a laser or a torch.

One of the creatures speeded up, still running straight at him. Moody searched the ground for a weapon, a rock or a stick or a club, but the soft ground held nothing except the remains of the immature corn crop.

Balling his fist, Moody stood his ground as the creature launched itself at him. He ducked and then dived out of the way, rolling once and coming up on his feet. The native hit the ground flat and seemed to be momentarily stunned. Moody leaped on its back, the heel of his left foot coming down at the base of the creature's skull. He heard bone snap. The creature bucked once, screamed, and was still.

Moody jumped away and turned, only to be hit in the head with a club. In the last instant, before it struck, he had seen it coming and had tried to duck. He'd been too slow. He saw an explosion of bright white and was aware of sounds around him as he collapsed.

Martha was caught before she was halfway to the house. The creatures ran her down and clubbed her in the back of the head. She took a running step and pitched to the ground. She had tried to put her hands under her to push herself up but they would no longer obey her. She looked up and saw the creatures closing on the house. She tried to scream a warning to the children but her voice squeaked in her throat and almost no sound came out of her mouth.

When the creatures finished in the house, they came out, walking across the soft, plowed ground. One of them grabbed at Martha's arms and partially lifted her and then dragged her forward, toward where her husband lay.

Moody looked up as the native dropped the limp body of his wife near him. He thought, for the moment, that she was dead and then saw a spark of life in her eyes. A creature lifted its club and slammed it into her skull. There was a sickening snap of bone but no sound from her. She died in an instant.

And then he saw one of them moving toward him and knew what his fate was going to be. Looking at the bloody body of his wife, Moody knew that he didn't care.

Colonel David Jefferson lay on the tiny cot that could be pushed up into the bulkhead and wondered if there wasn't something that he should be doing. Something important. Something that had to do with the running of his regiment. He was sure there was, but at the moment couldn't think of what it might be. Not that he cared, at the moment.

He rolled to his side and put a hand under his head to support it and looked at the hatch. He should be up and moving. His executive officer, Major Victoria Torrence, would be looking for him soon. He grinned at the thought of her showing up at his hatch, entering and seeing him lying in bed. Maybe she'd strip off her uniform and climb in with him.

Jefferson shook his head and rolled to his back, throwing off the sheet. That was not the way he should be thinking of his executive officer even though she was willing to see him outside of duty hours, on a personal level. She had originally made the offer with the thought of keeping the battalion running smoothly. Jefferson hadn't liked the reason though he'd been in favor of the action.

Torrence, he thought, was weird in a professional way. She was a good soldier, an excellent tactician, and was ready to do everything she could to make sure the regiment ran smoothly. She was a young, good-looking woman who was smart enough to realize that sometimes personal feelings and beliefs had to be set aside for the greater good of the regiment.

And, she'd made the offer because Courtney Norris, Jefferson's supply officer, had been trying very hard to get him into bed. Torrence believed, and she could be right, that if Jefferson slept with the female members of the staff, other than herself, it might undermine his authority with the entire regiment.

Thinking about the two women who wanted to climb in the sack with him made Jefferson wish that he'd slept longer and been thinking about manifests or rosters or equipment problems. He got up, walked to the computer and typed in a message, waited, and then read the screen. There was nothing pressing until zero nine hundred ship time. An hour and a half.

He took a shower, ignoring the fact that the tepid water had been recycled a hundred times. He couldn't get it cold enough to solve his immediate problem. Images of both Torrence and Norris danced in his head and neither of them were in uniform. Neither of them were in anything, and that was the problem.

"The general staff," he said out loud. That was a way around the problem. The women members of the staff wouldn't present the problems that the women on his own staff did. Most of them were of equal rank and they were outside his immediate command.

Then, stepping from the shower, he realized that his thinking was wrong. He couldn't just leap the bones of anyone for the pure pleasure of leaping their bones. And then he thought that through and realized if the woman was a willing participant and understood the ground rules there would be no . . .

The chirping of the signal at his hatch drew his attention. He moved to the computer and touched the buttons. Torrence was standing there, in full uniform, staring up at the button camera, waiting.

Hitting the speaker, Jefferson said. "Give me a moment?"

"Yes, sir."

Jefferson grabbed some shorts and then put on his uniform

trousers. He pulled a T-shirt over his head and then touched the speaker. "Come on in."

Torrence opened the hatch, ducked, and stepped in. She looked at Jefferson and said, "I thought you were already awake."

"I was. I took a shower." He sat on the edge of his cot and picked up his socks.

Torrence looked at the chair bolted to the deck in front of the desk but didn't sit. Jefferson noticed that and waved to her, telling her to go ahead and sit.

"Got a message in, about fifteen minutes ago," she said.

Jefferson sat up and stared at her. He noticed that she was in her military role. Sometimes, when there was no one around, Torrence loosened up and kidded with him. But only if the military business had been taken care of for the day.

"Maybe you'd better give it all to me."

She shook her head. "I thought that when you got the regiment we'd be done with the chickenshit details. That as a regiment, we'd be above the police-action activities."

"I think," said Jefferson, "that I could be the commanding general of the entire army and there would be someone a step above me handing down the chickenshit."

"The message said that some colonists were having trouble with the local, indigenous populations. We are to send down a company—no more than a battalion—to handle the situation."

"Uh-huh," said Jefferson.

"Oh," said Torrence, "there is one other thing. We're getting a new platoon."

"What? You mean we're getting replacements?"

"No. We're getting a platoon. We're to attach it to one of the companies. It's an autonomous unit and will operate as a platoon assigned to a company."

"It don't think I like the sound of this."

Torrence stood and grinned. "Good morning, Colonel. Thought I'd brighten your day."

"You wait," said Jefferson, "until I finish dressing and we'll go get some breakfast."

"Yes, sir."

2

DEBARKATION CENTER, EARTH

THE PLATOON WAS lined up in three rows at the far end of the
spaceport. There were standing on the edge of the tarmac while
support vehicles darted in and out, taking supplies and equipment to the shuttle. The platoon didn't complain about the heat
or the humidity or the thick, smog-choked atmosphere. They
stood quietly, waiting for their orders, just as they had been
trained to do.

John, Six One Two, left Sara, Six One Three, in charge as
he walked into the closest building. It was a single-story
structure made of crumbling cinder blocks and rusting corru-
gated tin. The windows had been replaced with plywood and
the door had steel mesh over the window.

Inside there was a waist-high counter and, sitting behind it,
looking as if she had nothing at all to do, was a master
sergeant. She sat there, staring at the plywood-covered window, in the building that wasn't air-conditioned, and said
nothing at all. She didn't even look up as John, Six One Two,
entered.

"Sergeant," he said.

She turned slowly, looked at him, and said, "Good Christ,
they're getting younger every day."

"Sergeant, I have my platoon here and ready for transport to
the ship."

The sergeant sat for a moment, staring, and then said, "You have a designation?"

"Recon Platoon attached to the Tenth Interplanetary Infantry."

The sergeant turned, touched the keyboard of her computer, and said, "You're early."

"Yes."

"Two hours early. You'll have to amuse yourselves until it's time to process."

"Couldn't we do that early? Now? To get it out of the way."

"Processing begins in two hours," said the sergeant.

"I'd like to get it taken care of now, Sergeant," he said, stressing the word sergeant.

"I'm sure you would, but processing begins in two hours and that's when it will begin."

"I could make it an order."

"Well," she said, "I suppose you could, but then I'd have to point out that regulations dictate the processing and although it may look as if I have nothing to do, the scheduling must be maintained. If you have a problem with that, you take it up with Major Davidson in the headquarters building at the far end of the field."

John, Six One Two, stood there for a moment, the anger boiling through him. A sergeant had no business telling a lieutenant what she would do or wouldn't do. If the platoon was there, she should process it, not wait because the regulations said that she should. John, Six One Two, wanted to slam his fist onto the counter. He wanted to smash her face and make her do what he wanted. What good was being an officer if the NCOs and enlisted ranks ignored what he wanted?

And then it passed. The white flame of his anger burned out and he was left wishing that he had never come into the office. He was embarrassed by not being able to handle the sergeant any better than he had. Without a word, he turned and left the building. He walked back to the platoon and then looked beyond them to where there was a concrete wall topped with a sagging, rusting chain link fence.

"Sergeant," he said as he approached.

Sara, Six One Three, turned toward him and saluted. "Sir!"

John, Six One Two, stopped in front of her and looked down at the ground. "Let's put the platoon at rest. Have them fall out and let them congregate near the wall. We've a two-hour wait."

"Yes, sir."

She turned, calling them to attention, and then gave them their orders. When she had told them to fall out, they moved back to the wall, separating and spreading out.

John, Six One Two, stood watching for a moment and then followed. He sat down on the wall, his hands holding onto the sun-warm concrete and his feet drumming against it.

"Sir," said one of the women.

He looked at her. Shelia, Seven Four Eight, stood in front of him at attention. Sweat stained her grey flight suit. She had removed her helmet and sweat had beaded on her forehead and upper lip.

"What can I do for you?"

"Sir. How long are we going to have to wait here?"

"Two hours, until they are ready to process us."

"Sir. Can we go find something to eat and drink?"

"No. I think that we'd better just hang loose here in case they can get us in sooner."

"Yes, sir." She saluted, but John, Six One Two, could tell that she was angry.

David, Four Five Nine, appeared. He sat down and looked at the lieutenant. "We just have to wait here?"

"Yes. Just wait. We're early."

"You'd think that they could do a little better than that," said David, Four Five Nine. "Two hours is a long time to wait. Almost forever."

"It's only two hours," said John, Six One Two.

"Except when you're waiting. Then it's a long time."

"Sure."

John, Six One Two, watched as the men and women, his brothers and sisters, spread out, sat down, and stretched out using their duffel bags for pillows. A couple pulled comix from pockets and flipped through them. Another man sorted through his stuff until he found a handful of cards and moved toward Jane, Three Three Three. He sat down facing her, showed her the top card, and they began talking in low tones.

"Lieutenant," said Sara Six One Three, "isn't there some-thing that we can do?"

"No. I told you. We have to wait. That's all we can do now. Just wait."

"Yes, sir."

They sat quietly, watching the platoon. Some of them slept and some of them talked. They traded comix and cards and shared the little candy they had sneaked into their gear. They broke up into small groups, sticking together, not by squads or fire teams, but by some other criterion. The breakdown was not along military lines but along bloodlines in some fashion that John, Six One Two, didn't understand.

He had hoped, as the hypno tapes had suggested, that the fire teams and the squads would operate as a unit, sticking together even when outside the military umbrella. But there had also been a directive telling him that the oldest men and women should be given the positions of authority even when the differences in age were matters of minutes.

He had done what they wanted, but when the platoon was released from duty, they broke down in a way that defied explanation. They didn't do it by age or sex. They did it in some other way.

Molly, Eight One Nine, appeared and said, "I have to go to the bathroom."

"Can't you wait?"

"No."

John, Six One Two, wiped a hand over his face and looked at Sara, Six One Three. "Sergeant, check with the platoon and see who has to use the facilities and then march them over to the processing shed. See about finding a place for them."

"Yes, sir."

Sara, Six One Three, walked over to the waiting platoon and said, "Anyone need to hit the latrine?"

A couple of them stood up and moved forward. Two of them were holding hands, but it was a sign of affection between brother and sister and nothing more.

"Hurry it up," said John, Six One Two.

Those who had to go headed across the tarmac to the small building. John, Six One Two, didn't move. He sat there watching as a yellow vehicle worked its way across the ramp, toward a shuttle sitting to one side. Behind it was a giant hangar that dwarfed everything. Through the massive doors was another shuttle, the front under the cockpit removed as a dozen technicians worked on it.

Two of his sisters approached. "How much longer are we going to have to wait?"

John, Six One Two, looked at his watch. "I think we've waited about long enough." He glanced beyond them, at Susan, One One Four. He pointed at her, got her attention, and said, "Fall the troops in. Get them ready to move."

"Yes, sir."

Susan, One One Four, stepped forward and ordered the platoon to fall in. As she did, John, Six One Two, pushed himself off the wall and walked back toward the low building. Before he could reach the door, it opened and the sergeant stepped out. When she saw him, she waved at him, telling him it was time.

He turned and saw that the platoon, minus those who had gone in search of the latrine, was ready. Susan, One One Four, was watching him, waiting for orders.

"Get the platoon over there and wait," he said.

"Yes, sir."

As she moved the platoon out, John, Six One Two, hurried past them. He reached the door and looked the sergeant in the eye. "Is it time now?"

"Certainly, sir. Bring your people in and we'll get the processing completed."

"Thank you." He ducked back outside and watched as the platoon was marched toward him. Susan, One One Four, stopped them, turned them, and then moved closer to him.

As she did that, someone in the rear said, "I don't want to do this. It's not fun."

Two hours later they were on the shuttle, in orbit to rendezvous with the interstellar transport. The enlisted ranks were in the back, the NCOs in the middle, and John, Six One Two, was up front with a couple of officers from other units. The seats were plush and comfortable up front. In the rear they weren't quite as wide and there wasn't quite as much legroom. The cabin crew didn't get back there quite as often.

John, Six One Two, wasn't aware of all that. He sat quietly, watching the screen as first it showed the lift-off from Earth and the rapid climb through the atmosphere, and then switched to entertainment programming. It wasn't what he would have chosen had anyone asked, but it was better than tactical manuals and hypno tapes.

Sara, Six One Three, came forward and crouched in the aisle near him. She glanced at the captain in the closest seat and then ignored the man. To the lieutenant, she said, "I think you should come back for a few minutes."

"Why?"

"Just an appearance to settle the troops down. They're getting restless again."

John, Six One Two, understood the restlessness. He felt the same way. He wanted to get out of the seat, out of the shuttle, and run loose. He wanted to play a few games, drink a Coke or two, and not worry about the upcoming assignment or the trip to the regiment. He wished that he could just forget everything. All the responsibility and the authority, and have a good time.

But he was the officer in charge and could not show any of that. If the troops, when bored, pulled out their comix and cards and flopped down on the tarmac, he couldn't do it. That had been impressed on him. Lead by example if nothing else. Don't correct their minor actions but show them the way to act. Be the teacher through example.

So, they might be restless. But no more restless than he was. They might be uncomfortable, but no more uncomfortable. And now he had to head back there to nursemaid them because they weren't having the times of their lives.

"I'll be right there," he said.

"Yes, sir."

The captain unbuckled his seat belt and floated up, out of his seat, turning slightly so that John, Six One Two, could get up and out.

"That girl looks just like you," he said.

"My sister."

The captain shrugged. "I didn't think that they allowed members of the same family to serve in the same unit. Not after that Sullivan thing."

John, Six One Two, floated a foot or so above his seat. "What's the Sullivan thing?"

"During War Two the old United States Navy had five brothers from the same family serving on the same ship. All five were killed in the same action." The captain shook his head. "Quite a loss for a single family to bear. From that point, military regulations dictated that members of a family be spread out so that all of them won't get killed at once."

"Guess the regulations have changed," said John, Six One Two.

"Not that I'm aware of," said the captain. "You can't even get waivers for it, so I'm surprised that your sister is in the unit with you."

"We're noncombat," said John, Six One Two.

"Now you might be, but that's a situation that changes rapidly once you hit the frontier."

John, Six One Two, pushed himself clear and then reached up to touch the overhead. He pushed down and felt his feet contact the velcro aisle. He slipped along it, moving to the rear where his brothers and sisters waited. All forty-two of them, in the same platoon. He wondered about the five Sullivans, killed when their ship was sunk in War Two. He wondered why all his brothers and sisters were in the same platoon. And then he was among them, seeing them again, and the thoughts of the five Sullivans were pushed aside.

3

DELTA ROYAL THREE

"If we do not do something immediately, there will be mob rule," said Leigh Starling. "It's already beginning." She was a pleasant-looking woman with short brown hair and brown eyes. Her build would be called stocky, but it was more muscular than fat. There was a single, light scar on her cheek that was years old.

Thomas Nast, the colonial commissioner, sat at his desk and said, "What's happening?" Nast was a small man with greasy black hair, a long, pointed nose and small, brown eyes. He rarely smiled, but only because he didn't want his subordinates to know what he was thinking. He believed that the most disciplined organizations were ruled by fear. An employee afraid of the boss was no threat to the boss.

Starling shot a glance at Jeremy Clovers and said, "In the last twenty-four-hour period, there have been systematic attacks on the native villages by armed farmers and ranchers resulting in the deaths of four humans and fifty to sixty of the natives."

"Damn the natives," said Nast.

Clovers shook his head. Clovers was almost the opposite of Nast. He was tall and skinny with light hair and light-colored eyes. He was a good-natured man who was slow to anger and friendly with everyone.

Staring down at the table, Clovers said, "The problem is the escalating hostility between our people and the natives. If we ignore the property damage, which to this point has been fairly superficial, and concentrate only on the deaths and the time lost, we're already into a major problem financially."

Now they had Nast's attention. He didn't care if some of the natives were killed by angry humans. Hell, he didn't even care if some humans were killed by angry natives. There were hundreds, thousands, of colonists and if a family was killed, they were easy to replace. But lost time and crops were lost revenues and that was something the company would not tolerate. Any red ink on the balance sheet was cause for dismissal. A little red blood never hurt anyone.

Nast focused his attention on Clovers. "What's happening out there?"

"It looks as if the natives are beginning to rebel at the pressure from our expansion."

"They never cared before," said Nast. "We bargained with them and paid them for our intrusion."

"But I don't think they understood the concept," said Clovers.

"They were willing to take the money, or rather the goods, when offered."

Now Starling spoke up. "I think they thought of the goods as gifts. When the first of our people arrived, they didn't see them as a territorial threat. Now we've put up cities and homesteads and fences, and their access to lands and rivers that was once free and easy is now blocked."

"Oh, hell," said Nast, "what kind of bullshit are you handing out here?"

"That doesn't matter," said Clovers, putting a hand on Starling's arm to quiet her. "What does matter is that the natives are getting restless."

"We're not in an adventure video here," said Nast.

"But it applies. They're not happy and they're coming out of the forest to tear up crops and kill the farmers. Farmers are retaliating by hunting them."

Nast nodded and turned to the computer. He touched the keyboard and then rocked back to watch the screen. The words and numbers paraded over it. There was a moment when a graph grew on it, the bars winking in a variety of colors and then it disappeared, replaced by a pie chart.

"We are not in any difficulty now," said Nast.

"No, but we could be," said Starling. "We need to get some help in here."

"Help? From where?"

Starling shot a glance at Clovers. "There are provisions for protecting both the local populations and the humans. We should make a formal request."

"No," said Nast. "That's out." He rocked back and steepled his fingers under his chin. He was aware of the history of the regiments brought in to protect colonial interests. They weren't driven by the corporations. They were interested in protecting the people and the natives and didn't care about the bottom line. They would get in the way.

Starling took over. "This is a crisis that is building. We can stop it now with a little outside help."

"Ridiculous," said Nast.

"If you don't do something," said Clovers, "the farmers will. They're already talking of forming a militia."

Nast glanced again at the screen and then reached over to shut down the computer. To the two people, he said, "The formation of militias is as old as the human race. Whenever two or more people get together, they form a militia for the common good. I think it's a marvelous idea."

"But then they begin to talk about training and drills and finally someone decides that it's necessary to sally forth, attacking the common enemy."

"Still . . ." said Nast.

"It takes time away from their regular work," said Clovers. "And once one group forms a militia, the others will follow suit until we have armed camps all over the planet's surface."

"I have no problem . . ." started Nast.

"But if we make a call for a small force for protection, then we might avoid that." Starling's voice softened. "Production increases and everyone looks good."

"I suppose that I could put in a request for a temporary peace-keeping force."

"Yes," snapped Clovers. "Yes. And when things calm down, we can have them withdrawn."

"How soon?" asked Starling.

"Well . . ."

"We've got a situation developing here," she said. "We get in and move now, we can contain it. We let it go and we're going to be in trouble."

"Then I'll put in the request as soon as I can get it drawn," said Nast.

Starling got to her feet and nodded at him. "The sooner the better."

"So you said."

She waited for Clovers to stand and then said, "It's the right decision."

"I hope so, because if it's not, it'll be on my head and not yours."

Jefferson sat in his conference room and looked at Torrence and then at Captain Linda Martuesi. Both were dressed in dark uniforms with the blue piping of the Tenth Interplanetary Infantry. Martuesi was a small woman with black hair, olive skin and deep brown eyes. She had only recently joined the regiment and was the junior company commander.

Both women sat at the sides of the table, one opposite the other with Jefferson at the head. There was a file folder with hard copy sitting in front of him and a computer with a printer at his side.

"Major," he said, addressing Torrence. "You'll be taking what amounts to a light battalion in. Two companies and a headquarters platoon."

"You've selected the units?" asked Martuesi.

Jefferson glanced at her but didn't answer the question. Instead he turned his attention back to Torrence. "I want you in command of it, but allow the company commanders to operate independently."

"Yes, sir."

"Martuesi, I asked you here so that you would know that giving tactical command to Major Torrence did not reflect on you. I wanted a senior officer in charge."

"What about Garvey?" asked Torrence.

"I don't think I'll mention this to Garvey. We'll just detach the people and let it go at that."

"Too late, Colonel," said Torrence. "Garvey already asked if he could go along."

Jefferson shook his head. "I don't like that."

"The people have a right to know," said Torrence.

"Who's Garvey?" asked Martuesi.

Jefferson rubbed his chin and then said, "Our representative of the Fourth Estate." To Torrence he said, "How in the hell did he hear about this?"

"I don't know, but he did point out that we haven't done anything of interest in the last few weeks. He's tired of making tapes for the Home Town Release Service. There are only so many times he can stomach one of our men or women telling friends and family about the great adventure."

Jefferson turned to the computer and typed for a moment. He sat back and let the data scroll across the screen. "I can't see anything here that's going to come back to haunt us. Hell, let Garvey go."

"Yes, sir."

He rocked back and looked at Martuesi and then at Torrence. "Take Crommel's company too but leave him here. I'll assign him to a staff job and bump Sinclair up to acting exec."

"That seems to be a lot of trouble," said Torrence.

"Having the people get the experience now is better than having to force someone into a position in a combat situation. Gives everyone a chance to learn without pressure."

"Sir," said Martuesi, "I haven't had a chance to learn anything except in the hypno tanks."

"That's why you're going and not someone else," said Jefferson. He turned his attention to Torrence, "We've got that special platoon coming in. I thought I'd deploy them with you."

"Before you have the chance to look them over?" asked Torrence.

"Colonel Prescott gave me a good briefing on the situation," said Jefferson. "I got with Carter," he glanced at Martuesi, "he's the S-2, and had him give me a rundown on this. What we've got here is a policing action. We're not going to run into anything too tough."

"Then why am I going?" asked Torrence.

Jefferson shook his head slowly as if she'd asked an incredibly stupid question. "Napoleon said that an army moved on its stomach but he was wrong. It moves on paperwork and filling the proper squares. Now, when promotion time rolls around, wouldn't you like to have some independent command time filling some of those squares?"

"Yes, sir."

"Then that's what we'll do." He sat back, away from the table. "Questions?" When neither of them spoke, he said, "Then we'll try for launch of the independent companies in fifteen days. That give you the time?"

Martuesi came to her feet. "Yes, sir. Plenty." She saluted and then whirled, marching from the conference room.

"Young, isn't she?" said Torrence.

Jefferson stared at the hatch. "Aren't we all young?"

Torrence nodded. "Yeah. Maybe I meant immature."

"I'm not sure that I should comment on that either," said Jefferson.

"Hell, Colonel, you were both young and immature when you came on board but what the hell did anyone expect?"

Jefferson said, "Yeah, what?" but he knew. He'd just been handed the biggest prize in the army. They'd decided that he should get the Galactic Silver Star though he tried to tell them that Sergeant Mason deserved it. He didn't know that the army preferred live heros to dead ones. Live heros tended to inspire the living while dead heros were just dead. So they'd pinned the medal on him, or rather, hung it around his neck, promoted him and handed him a battalion although he hadn't been competent enough to command a platoon.

"We give her a chance to learn the job where no one is going to die."

"If it's that safe," said Torrence, "why is everyone so hot to get us there? Why not take a month to prepare everything properly?"

"Because," said Jefferson grinning broadly, "our operational plans suggest that we can field the regiment in twenty-four hours. Therefore we should be able to field a modified and light battalion in that time."

Torrence got to her feet. "Then I'd better get busy, hadn't I?"

"Vicky," said Jefferson.

She waited for him to speak and finally asked, "What?"

"There have been rumors . . ."

"Yes. I know."

"Well, not really rumors since they're basically true, but it's not good."

"So you're going to send me to some second-rate planet to stop the rumors."

Jefferson shrugged and said, "It's not second rate. More like third rate, but I think that'll slow things down. By the time you get back, they'll have something else to talk about so they can leave us alone."

Torrence glanced at the hatch and then at Jefferson. "We don't have much time. I'll need some in-depth briefings before I can take off."

Jefferson wanted to say that all the briefings had been arranged. He wanted to be able to tell her that they had to be careful in front of the troops, but all that vanished in a second. To her he said, "Yes, you'll need some personal instruction."

And then the hatch opened again and Garvey stuck his face in. He was wearing a grey flight suit with half a dozen patches from various units sewn on it. "Colonel," he said. "Can I speak to you?"

Jefferson fell back in his chair, rolled his eyes at Torrence and then said, "Sure." To Torrence, he said, "I'll see you later."

"Yes, sir."

As she left, Jefferson asked Garvey, "What can I do for you?"

"I just wanted to get the logistics of this thing worked out before we deploy."

Jefferson knew that it wouldn't be a quick meeting and suddenly he was relieved. "All right, Mister Garvey, let's get at it."

4

ABOARD THE SS *CLIFFORD McKLUSKY*

IT WAS THE first time that John, Six One Two, had found himself sharing a room with another. During his childhood and training, as the only officer, he had been granted quarters to himself. He had learned the privileges of rank early, getting his meals first, getting better meals, getting the single room, getting the privacy that the others were denied.

The senior sergeants of the platoon, Sara, Six One Three, and the squad leaders were housed together. The squads were quartered together, the bunk assignments dictated by membership in a specific squad or fire team. Squad leaders could bunk with their squads or in the senior NCO billets.

But all of them had roommates. Everyone found himself or herself in with another group of people. Everyone except John, Six One Two. Now, on the ship, where space was limited and there were no luxury accommodations for junior officers, John, Six One Two, found himself in with three other lieutenants, two female and one male.

John, Six One Two, sat on his cot, and watched as the other three came and went. He sat with his duffel bag shoved up close, his right foot on it, as if afraid they were going to steal it or search it.

One of the women entered, glanced at him and then turned her back. She stripped her uniform, then her underwear, and grabbed a towel. John, Six One Two, stared at her. He'd never seen a naked woman before, except his sisters. Suddenly he wanted to learn if the anatomy of other women matched that of his sisters.

She turned and saw him sitting there, staring. "You got a problem?"

"No. Just looking."

She continued to stare for a moment and then laughed. Turning slowly like a model on a stage, she asked, "You like what you see?"

John, Six One Two, studied the point between her legs. More hair there. And then he looked up at the breasts. Larger, rounder, with more nipple than his sisters. Same basic package with a few minor variations in the trim.

"Well?"

"Very nice," said John, Six One Two.

"Nice my ass. It's great." She stepped closer, stuck out a foot and posed in front of him, daring him to touch her. "Generals have been known to follow me."

He shrugged. Now that he had the answer to his question, he wasn't that interested any more. She looked just like his sisters. And he imagined the men would look just like his brothers. Not that he ever doubted it. It was just nice to have visual proof that he was right.

The woman spun again and picked up her towel, wrapping it around her so that her breasts and pubic area were covered. She glanced at him and said, "I don't think I care for the way you stare."

John, Six One Two, shrugged. He didn't know what to say to her. She was not a sister, an NCO, or an enlisted soldier. She held the same rank.

Without a word she stepped into the tiny alcove that served as a shower. She hung the towel up, closed the plastic door and turned on the water.

John, Six One Two, laid back on his cot, his hands under his head as he stared up at the overhead. A plain white overhead of molded plastic. He wasn't thinking about the woman or anything else, actually. He was letting his mind drift from thing to thing.

There was a quiet chirping at the hatchway. He didn't bother with it. A moment later the hatch opened and another officer stepped in. She was taller, blonder, and skinnier than the one in the shower. Glancing at her epaulets, he noticed the bars of a captain. Without thinking, he climbed to his feet.

"Ah, Lieutenant Smith," she said. "I'm Captain Scully."

"Captain." He remained standing.

"I'm afraid that you were assigned here by mistake. Your quarters are on the next deck down."

"I don't mind it here," said John, Six One Two.

"Well, your platoon is down there and we try to keep members of the same organization together. The lieutenants assigned to this room, for example, are replacements. They'll be stuck in various regiments as the need arises. You have an assignment already."

"Yes, ma'am."

"Grab your gear and I'll escort you to your new quarters."

John, Six One Two, crouched, pulled his duffel bag from under his cot and said, "I'm ready."

The shower door opened and the lieutenant stepped naked into the room. She pulled her towel down and began drying herself. She ignored both John, Six One Two, and Captain Scully.

"I'm ready."

Scully faced him and then nodded. She moved to the hatch, opened it, and stepped out into the companionway. John, Six One Two, followed.

John, Six One Two, left his new quarters which held a single cot, a single shower, and a computer terminal tied into the ship's mainframe. It was larger than the cabin he'd shared with the three lieutenants for a few hours.

He walked down the wide companionway that held armed soldiers every fifty feet. He was sure they were for show but it served as a constant reminder that they were heading to the frontier and that there were hostiles on the frontier. He didn't believe that any of them were spacefaring races but that didn't mean there might not be a sudden encounter.

The platoon had been quartered in a large bay. All four squads were there. Sara, Six One Three, and the four squad leaders had a cabin off the squad bay that allowed them some privacy. The gear had been stored in a bay off the main cabin. Everything they had was where they could get at it. Contact with the rest of the ship, with the crew, and with other soldiers was limited.

John, Six One Two, stopped outside the hatch, brushed at the front of his uniform and then touched the button. The hatch irised open and he stepped into a wall of noise.

The platoon was there. All of them except the senior sergeants. The deck was littered. Cots were overturned. Equipment, clothing, trash was spread everywhere. Members of the platoon were sprawled on the deck laughing helplessly. Others were wrestling. A female lay with her hands tied behind her. A male was lashed to a cot.

For an instant, John, Six One Two, wanted to join them. He wanted to leap into the fun, toss papers into the air, tackle one of the running men. And then his training kicked in. Images flashed in his mind. Lectures swelled, telling him to lead by example. Show the enlisted troops how they were to behave. He stood near the hatch and didn't utter a word.

Slowly, one by one, the platoon members spotted him and fell silent. They came to attention and failed to move again. No one shouted a warning, no one called the bay to attention. Each of them, as they spotted the lieutenant, realized they were in trouble and stopped moving.

Silence descended over the bay. John, Six One Two, his hands clasped behind his back, strolled in, glancing right and left, his feet rustling the papers. He looked down at the girl whose hands were tied and noticed that her feet were bound too. She couldn't move.

He spotted Molly, Eight One Nine. She was an assistant squad leader, the senior person he'd seen. "What in the hell is going on here?"

Molly, Eight One Nine, stood mute. There was nothing she could say.

John, Six One Two, rubbed a hand over his eyebrows, looking as if he'd eaten his ice cream too fast. "We finally get away from the Training Center and you think it is an excuse to rip apart your quarters?"

"No, sir."

He turned and looked at the others. "I don't understand this. We are highly trained individuals. We are supposed to be responsible adults. And you revert to such childish behavior the first chance you get." He whirled and stared at Molly, Eight One Nine.

"No excuse, sir."

"That's not going to cut it." He surveyed the squad bay. "Where are the squad leaders?"

"I don't know, sir."

"This squad bay will be cleaned," he said, his voice rising. "All equipment will be repaired and all gear will be stored. You will be ready for an inspection in two hours and I don't want to see a trace of the debris scattered here. Full inspection in proper uniform. Is that understood?"

"Yes, sir," said Molly, Eight One Nine.

He looked at the others. "Understood?"

"Yes, sir." It was a mumbled response but he let it go.

Turning to leave, he said, "I want to see you in the corridor now."

"Yes, sir."

John, Six One Two, exited then. He stopped just outside the hatch and waited. As Molly, Eight One Nine, joined him, he saw the platoon bend slowly to work. One boy scraping the papers together while two others righted a cot.

"Sir?"

"Just what in the hell was going on in there?"

"Sir?"

"Don't give me that crap. You're an NCO. You let them fall apart. Run wild."

Molly, Eight One Nine, stared at the deck. "Yes, sir. it was . . . I just . . ."

"What?"

"Well, I thought I should let them blow off a little steam. We haven't had much fun since the Training Center. Always been go go go. We've had to sit around in shuttles, or spaceports, waiting for someone to do something. I just thought that we could have a little fun."

"That was excessive. We have to remember that we are a military unit. We are not here to have fun."

"Yes, sir."

"I'm very disappointed in you," said John, Six One Two.

"There were other assistant squad leaders there too."

John, Six One Two, nodded. "You're right, and they all should be here. But they're not. I want you to see that the

platoon is ready for inspection. You are to alert the senior
NCOs and see that they get here too. Clear?"

"Yes, sir."

"You have something you want to say?"

"This isn't fair," said Molly, Eight One Nine.

"Not fair? How is it not fair?"

She shrugged. "The others aren't out here."

"I'll remember that they were in there too. You aren't the
only one in trouble over this. Everyone is in trouble."

"Yes, sir."

John, Six One Two, rubbed a hand through his hair. "You
get them ready. We have a good inspection and all this will be
forgotten."

"Yes, sir."

John, Six One Two, along with Sara, Six One Three, walked
among the members of the platoon. They had cleaned the
squad bay, straightened the bunks, and stored their gear. Each
was dressed in a clean fatigue uniform. They stood at rigid
attention, each afraid to move.

John, Six One Two, walked rapidly, glancing right and left,
looking for a sign they had failed in their task. When he spotted
nothing, he turned and left the squad bay, with Sara, Six One
Three, right behind him.

Outside, with the hatch closed, he asked, "Where were you
while they were tearing things apart?"

"We were coordinating with the galley crew for messing the
platoon and we were scheduling the training areas for the next
two weeks. I can't remain here day and night to make sure that
others are doing their jobs."

John, Six One Two, was going to respond and then realized
that his criticism of her could be directed at him. He hadn't
been watching them either, though he was the one that stopped
them.

"They're young," said Sara, Six One Three. "So very
young. They need time . . ."

"They're really no younger than us. Hours at the most," he
reminded her.

She grinned. "Responsibility teaches maturity. We have the
responsibility. They don't."

"They don't have to act like children," he said. "They

continue and we'll all find ourselves being treated like children."

She nodded. "Yes, sir."

"Okay," he said. He looked down at her and suddenly the image of the lieutenant who had displayed herself for him popped into this mind. He forced it down and asked, "You have trouble getting everything set?"

"No, sir. We have access to the mess area thirty minutes before everyone else. We'll be in and out before any of the others get there."

"I'll want to see a training schedule in the morning," he said.

"Yes, sir." She hesitated and then asked, "Off the record?"

"What?"

"You need to lighten up. We're all family here. They're your brothers and sisters."

"I know that. Maybe that's why I'm so angry. I expect something more of them. We're all the same person."

"Not quite," she said. "Besides, you're the oldest. You're just a little ahead of the rest of us."

"What do you think about what happened?" he asked. "About what they did?"

"I'm disappointed, but I understand it. Hell, if things were different, I might have joined in. They didn't really do anything that disastrous or destructive."

John, Six One Two, grinned. "I know. I felt the same way and that's what scared me."

5

DELTA ROYAL THREE

NAST, AGAINST HIS better judgment, had called for help and had been told that it would be a couple of weeks before anyone could get there. Nast figured that gave him time to solve the problem himself. If he could end it before the military arrived, his stock would rise.

Now, standing in front of him was a big man. He was a young man with dark hair and a scar on his face. It looked as if a small portion of his chin was missing. His hands were large and dirty, the fingernails caked. He wore ripped, dirty coveralls and had captain's bars pinned to the collar. He carried an old-fashioned rifle that had a magazine sticking out of the bottom. Nast wondered where he'd managed to find the captain's bars.

"I got two dozen men signed up right now. They're willin' to make a move."

Nast sat quietly, glancing at the computer screen, and said nothing to encourage the man.

"We're ready to move. All we want is a promise that our farms'll be looked after."

"Just what are you planning to do?"

"We're going hunting. I know where the bastards live and we plan to root them out of there. Only fair. They killed the Moodys and the Keys and then the Johnsons. Only fair."

Nast took a deep breath. "We've signed a treaty here. There is supposed to be no armed aggression. We're not supposed to be armed." He frowned at the rifle.

"We've got the right to protect ourselves."

Nast nodded. "I'd have to agree with that."

"All we want is the opportunity. Farms'll pretty well take care of themselves. All's we want is a commission to act for the colonial government. An official approval for our actions and a guarantee that there'll be no sanctions against us."

"Mister?"

"Captain," said the man. "Captain O'Neill. Been here for two years now."

"All right, Captain O'Neill. I must remind you that we have signed treaties with the locals."

"And they still attack. I figured that a little show of power, what we can do, will take the starch out of them."

Nast looked down at the computer, read the information on the screen, scrolled down for a few moments and then looked up. "I don't want a wholesale slaughter. I don't want you laying waste to the land but I do want these raids stopped. The sooner the better."

"We can do it," said O'Neill.

"You check with me later this afternoon and I'll have the documents drawn up and encoded for the computers and for transmission." Nast stared up at the man. "Who'll be the leader?"

"I will be," said O'Neill. "We had an election and I won it, fair and square."

"Fine. Weapons?"

"Each man supplies his own. We got enough. Need ammo. Figured you fellows should pay for the ammo." He hesitated and added. "Same with food and supplies, but I think you guys would want to pay for that."

"There is an operating budget that can be tapped," said Nast. "Your expenses will be covered."

"How many men?" asked O'Neill.

"What?"

"How many men will you finance on this?"

Nast looked down at the computer screen. The locals rarely congregated in groups larger than twenty or twenty-five except on rare occasions when everyone in a region met for a big, midsummer get-together. Then thousands got together on the banks of one of the larger rivers, fished, hunted, and sat around their campfires for a week, ten days, and then dispersed.

Of course, they didn't have firearms, they didn't understand rudimentary military tactics, and they didn't seem to operate well together in large groups. Knowing that, Nast said, "I don't want to see more than one hundred men involved in this. There is too much real work to be done."

"Nothing that can't wait a week or so. Besides, the damage done by these creatures cuts into the profits."

Nast rocked back in his chair and wished that the air-conditioner worked a little better. He was slightly uncomfortable. Rubbing a hand over his face, he said, again, "I don't want a wholesale slaughter. Just a punitive raid, maybe, directed specifically at the locals attacking us."

"Sure." O'Neill nodded.

"Then I'll see you this afternoon."

O'Neill exited the molded plastic building, into the almost blinding sunlight of late morning. He stood, a hand to shield his eyes, and saw Jason Becker sitting in the passenger's seat of the ATV. His rifle sat in the back. The windshield was mud-splattered and cracked.

"How'd it go?" asked Becker as O'Neill approached.

O'Neill studied the man. He was small, thin, balding, and bearded. He wore a faded blue work shirt and blue jeans, imported at great cost. Becker preferred them to the standard issue. He viewed them as a status symbol. The newer colonists couldn't afford the luxury of the imported work clothes.

O'Neill climbed behind the wheel and started the engine. Naturally it burned a methane derivative and not gasoline. He turned and looked at Becker and then grinned slowly. "He bought it. Gonna finance us. Few bucks for our time, supplies, and ammo."

"Yeah," said Becker. "About time."

O'Neill worked the gears, backed up, and then stopped in the center of the mud street. They splashed down it, to the end and stopped in front of another molded plastic building. The ground floor housed a bar. In the Old West it would have been a saloon. The interior was not dark, but brightly lighted. The furniture was plastic, molded from the same local materials as the walls and floor and ceiling. Everything inside was molded plastic, including the bar itself.

O'Neill pointed at a table and said, "Sit. I'll get the beer."

He bought two bottles and carried them to the table. He handed one to Becker and said, "You get with Peterson, Crawford and Portez. I want each of them to recruit five others. I want a list of names by the end of the day. I want one hundred men on the list."

"Women?" asked Becker.

O'Neill grinned. "You find a woman who wants in on this and she's in. Why the hell not?"

"Then what?" asked Becker.

O'Neill lowered his voice, though there was no one around to overhear them. "We go out to that little village about a dozen klicks from here and show them what a real raid is like. Nothing left standing. Nothing at all."

Jefferson was sitting in his small office, the computer screen in front of him glowing. He'd tapped into the ship's library and was reading a novel, but that was the thing about computers. If you were intently studying the screen, everyone assumed that you were engaged in real work. No one suspected that you were goofing off.

Torrence knocked on the bulkhead and stuck her head in. "You have a moment, sir?"

"Come on in."

She slipped into the plastic chair pushed back into a corner and crossed her legs. "We're getting close." She saw the look on his face, and added, "Delta Royal System."

"Ah. How go the preparations?"

"We're set. Martuesi has been doing the real work. Exercises with her troops and the second company. Search and destroy . . ."

"That the proper technique here?"

"Well, maybe not the destroy part," said Torrence. "More of a patrol. Show the colors and the weapons. A show of force."

Jefferson glanced at the novel and hit a key. The screen cleared except for the cursor flashing in the upper left-hand corner.

"How long to planetfall?"

"Ninety-six hours at the soonest. I'd be happier with a hundred and sixty-eight."

Jefferson knew that he'd been letting it slip. This was an action that didn't appeal to him. He'd palmed it off on Torrence and Martuesi, figuring they could handle it and he wouldn't be bothered. But he'd let them take too much of the responsibility.

"Any more communications with the colonial administration?"

"They haven't canceled the request, though they haven't been exactly thrilled that we're getting close."

"No need to rush?" asked Jefferson.

"They haven't indicated that things are slipping away from them."

"Then take your week. We'll establish an orbit. If they want us sooner, we'll be in a position to land. If not, make sure that you and Martuesi are ready before you deploy."

"Of course."

"You get with Intelligence and have them get you something on this place."

"Already done. Not much there. Out-of-the-way planet used mainly to support work on other worlds. There are probably ten, twelve thousand humans living there now, with a monthly increase of fifty to a hundred."

"Locals?" asked Jefferson.

Torrence straightened up. "Locals," she repeated. "Population, by our estimates, two million, two hundred thousand, scattered all over the planet's surface. Our estimates are that the planet, without outside assistance, is capable of supporting upwards of seven billion individuals. There should be no population pressures, either on us by them, or on them by us."

"So we've some unhappy natives attacking our people. Anyone know why?"

Torrence shrugged. "A farmer decided that the best land available was on a location that the locals considered sacred. The locals responded with an attack."

"Except there have been communications between us and them. No reason for an attack. Besides, we've carefully negotiated everything with them. This isn't like the expansion of the United States in the nineteenth century."

"Doesn't matter the reasons," said Torrence. "We'll just

land, end the problems, and see that there are no new ones cropping up. Simple."

Jefferson stood. "Sure. Simple."

Torrence didn't move. "One last item, Colonel."

"Yes."

"That new platoon. They should be arriving here in the next seventy-two hours."

"You get anything else on them? Anything that we don't already know?"

Torrence shook her head. "Courier brought a package with training records. They've been in intensive training for about a year, year and a half. Hypno, tapes, subliminal, everything. They've trained the officer in his role, the NCOs in theirs, and the enlisted in theirs. Enlisted didn't receive any officer material and the officer received nothing from the enlisted point of view."

"I'm not sure I like that. Doesn't hurt for the officers to understand the enlisted mind. Hell, it helps for the enlisted troops to understand the officers."

"New training regimen," said Torrence. "This is an experimental group. I would imagine that if it is successful, they'll begin to train more soldiers this way."

"The old Soviet Army thought that way. The enlisted troops were there to serve. To obey orders. American philosophy was to train everyone to think. Marines of the old American military establishment were particularly good at that. In some battles, PFCs and corporals ended up as company commanders because all those above them had been killed or wounded."

"Still, you have to try new things. Sometimes the old ways aren't always the best. They're just the oldest," said Torrence. "Besides, we haven't run into a situation in a hundred years where the command structure has been so badly chopped up. Radio links and computer coding have made command and control a much better proposition."

"Sometimes the old ways are the best." He glanced at the clock on the bulkhead above the hatch and watched as is snapped from eleven fifty-nine to twelve noon. "You ready for lunch?"

"Sure. Always."

"When we're finished, I think I'll want to read that report on this new platoon. I think they should deploy with you, but I want to be sure."

"Certainly."

Jefferson closed the hatch behind him and glanced down the corridor. Armed soldiers stood at regular intervals. It was a training maneuver. Let them learn about guard duty aboard the ship where a screw-up wouldn't cost them their lives. They knew that aggressors, appointed by either him or Torrence, would periodically try to penetrate the area. Once every two or three weeks it would happen. Just often enough to keep them on their toes.

They reached the mess facility and joined the line there. It looked as if Company B of the Second Battalion had just arrived. Jefferson could see no reason to push forward since they weren't on a tight schedule. Besides, it did the troops good to see the colonel in the line with them. Proved to them that he was a regular guy. He didn't take advantage of his position or his rank.

"So," said Torrence. "Here we are."

Jefferson knew that she was just making conversation. Making noise, but he didn't feel like responding. He was thinking about that new platoon. He was thinking about who they were and what kind of intensive training they'd had. Suddenly, he didn't like the concept. Thought that it was something that was going to haunt them once the platoon arrived. He didn't know why he felt that way, only that he did.

6

DELTA ROYAL THREE

CAPTAIN RICHARD O'NEILL stood in front of his makeshift army and stared at them, waiting for them to fall silent. It was what John Wayne did on the old videos. Stand in front of the soldiers and outwait them.

The soldiers of his ragtag army stood in a loose formation. They were armed with hunting rifles, shotguns, revolvers, and a few military weapons. There were no laser rifles or beam weapons.

O'Neill finally ran out of patience and said, "Will you people shut the fuck up."

"Yes, sir," screamed a voice from the rear.

O'Neill searched for the voice but failed to find it. Instead he stared at the eight-five men and seventeen women. "This is going to be a military organization. We have a military job to do and we are going to act like the military."

The voice said, "What the fuck do you know about the military?"

Now O'Neill knew who it was. He moved among the soldiers, shouldered his way to the rear rank and stood staring down at Clarence Ellis. He was a little man who always had something mean to say. He hated everyone and everything and wasn't happy unless he was putting down everything.

"You have a question?" said O'Neill, his voice low.

"Nope. Nothing at all."

O'Neill stood for a moment as if trying to figure out what to do. Finally he lifted his hand and pointed. "Why don't you just get the hell out of here? We have work to do and we don't need you."

"I'll stay."

O'Neill seemed to swell. "That was not a request. Get the hell out of here. NOW!"

Ellis didn't move for a moment. He glanced right and left, saw that everyone was watching him. Finally he shrugged and stepped back, away from O'Neill. He turned and began to walk away, but stopped suddenly. "I'll get you," he said.

"Sure," said O'Neill. "You've got me scared." O'Neill moved back to the front and asked, "Anyone else have any comments they'd care to make?"

"Yeah," said a man. "What about Ellis's question? What background do you have?"

O'Neill stared, but the tactic didn't work with the new man. "Okay," said O'Neill, "I had some training on Earth before I shipped out here. And I've reviewed a number of the manuals available in the computer library. Anyone else have any training at all?"

No one volunteered.

O'Neill grinned. "Then if there is no one else with any training and no one objects, I will continue in my role as the captain of this unit."

When no one objected, he continued. "Jason Becker will be the first lieutenant, Robert Jones the second lieutenant and Preston Pruggs is the first sergeant." He glanced at the rear and added, "I'll want Helen Byrd as a lieutenant in charge of the women."

"When we going to do something except stand around here and play soldier?" shouted a man.

"Yeah," agreed a second.

O'Neill nodded at them. "I understand your concern. These . . . creatures . . . have been tearing up our crops and attacking our people. You know it and I know it, even if those dummies in the colonial office don't know it. You want to act."

"Damn straight."

"You people ready to go tonight?"

"Yeah!" shouted a half dozen.

O'Neill fumbled with a pocket, pulled a computer printout from it and held it up like a banner. "This is our commission. We have been duly appointed by the representatives of our government on this planet. We have been tasked with ending the destruction of our crops and the attacks on our fellows."

There was a shout from the men and women standing in front of him. It started as a quiet cheer that built slowly, like a distant train. Suddenly it was a roar of approval. One man pointed his rifle into the air and pulled the trigger. Others joined in and there was a rippling of gunfire.

O'Neill stood there for a moment, watching. He lifted his hands, just as he'd seen politicians on the videos, and waited for silence. When the cheering subsided, he asked in a quiet voice, "You ready to go tonight?"

"Yeah."

"Right now."

"Good," said O'Neill, "Because I've a plan. I've talked about it with Becker and Pruggs and they like it." He searched the faces of the assembled mob. "You want to hear it?"

Again there was a cheer. O'Neill couldn't help smiling. He knew these people, knew what it would take to get their attention and hold it. They didn't want to hear about how the locals were intelligent creatures. They didn't want to hear talk of restraint and of patrolling the area to keep the locals from infiltrating. They wanted to make a positive move. They wanted to go out in search of the enemy and kill him, just as the enemy had done to their fellows on half a dozen occasions.

"There is a village not more than fifteen klicks from here situated on the New Mississippi. Becker's seen it. Been there and looked it over. Becker."

The first lieutenant, still dressed in his blue jeans and blue work shirt, but now with a single silver bar denoting his rank pinned to the collar, stepped forward. He looked at the men and women and wanted to crouch on the ground to draw in the dirt just as he'd seen others do in the videos. Generals sketching their battle plans for the troops.

Instead he stood and said, "You all know that big loop in the Mississippi north of here. Looks kind of like the top of a giant mushroom?" He didn't wait for an answer. "Village is situated in the tip of it. Water on three sides. Good bottomland that we can't get because them creatures live there. And, near as I can tell, that's where the raiders live."

"Details," said O'Neill.

Becker looked at him and nodded. "There's twenty-five or thirty mud huts. There's a couple of community houses. Big things in the center, maybe two stories high. Thatch type roofs. They got a few rudimentary streets of mud and let the animals run wild. There's a square in the middle where they have, what . . ." He shrugged. "Hell, some kind of market. Open air with wooden and mud stalls. Nothing fancy."

"Defenses?"

"Hell, couple of mud walls here and there, but I don't think they're defenses," said Becker.

"How many live there?" asked another.

"Not many. A dozen families but they've got fifteen or twenty big bucks. They're dangerous."

"That," said O'Neill, "should be our target. Unless there are any objections."

"We know for certain that those who attacked are from that village?"

"Village?" said O'Neill. "You say village. It's just a collection of huts. Not a village. It's the closest so I guess they came from there."

"I don't know," said a voice. "I should think we'd want to be correct."

O'Neill lifted a hand and waved it. "Enough talk. Let's hit the vehicles and get out there. Once we show them a little power, they'll stop attacking us."

He stood still, waiting, hoping they'd follow. Then one man cheered and another broke ranks. They swarmed forward, surrounding him for a moment and then pushing beyond, to the array of ATVs. They boarded, five, six and sometimes seven in a vehicle.

O'Neill, along with Becker, walked toward the lead ATV. Becker climbed behind the wheel and O'Neill stepped up on the passenger's seat. He turned, grabbed the roll bar and faced the assembled mass. A couple of men scrambled over the rear to sit in the backseat. O'Neill waved a hand like a wagon master starting the journey across the Great Plains.

Engines roared to life. A couple belched clouds of black smoke, but most burned the clean methane. O'Neill stood for a moment as Becker dropped his vehicle into gear. As they bounced across the open ground, O'Neill turned and sat down.

"Figure it'll take us about an hour to get there."

"About," agreed Becker.

O'Neill glanced into the back seat. "Pruggs, I think maybe you'd better take about a dozen guys and set up on the far side of that camp. We'll come at them across the river, shooting, and drive them into you."

"How deep's the river?" asked Pruggs.

O'Neill looked at Becker. "Well?"

"This time of year, no more than four feet and probably not that. We haven't had a good downpour in what, ten days or two weeks?"

"You circle around," said O'Neill, "and set up to block them. We'll hit them about dawn."

"Who do we shoot?" asked Pruggs. "Kids?"

"Hell," said O'Neill. "Nits make lice. We wipe them out."

They parked the ATVs in the woods and then crept through the trees to the edge of the river. They spread out there, slipping closer to the water. O'Neill ordered Becker and then Jones to take men both far to the right and far to the left. He'd attack up the middle with the main body as Becker and Jones hit the sides, funneling the creatures back, toward Pruggs. They'd have the enemy surrounded and they'd be able to kill them all.

O'Neill stretched out on the damp ground and watched the darkened camp. He could hear the water from the river. There was a quiet call from a bird. A few insects twilled and something screamed in the distance.

Becker dropped to the ground next to him. "I think everyone's in place."

"Good. Now, all we have to do is wait quietly until first light. They won't know what hit them."

"Why first light?"

"Let's us see what we're doing," said O'Neill. "I'd like to hit them now, but in the dark some of them might escape. We don't want that."

"I guess not."

O'Neill slipped to the rear and let the branches of a fern-like plant shield him. He stared at Becker, the face of his friend barely visible in the dark. Lowering his voice, he said, "This will teach them a lesson. One they've got to learn. It's like sticking your dog's nose in the mess he's made. You don't want to do it, don't want to punish him, but you have to."

"And once he's learned his lesson," said Becker.

"Once he's learned who's boss," amended O'Neill, "then things go back to the way they were."

Becker fell silent. O'Neill rolled to his belly and laid his head on his hands. He could feel the dampness seeping through his overalls. He could smell the rotting vegetation and the decaying fish. That was the thing he didn't like about the river. The disgusting odors surrounding it. But it was a hundred times better than the stench of the cities on Earth.

"I'd better get back to my men," said Becker.

O'Neill checked the time. "I think we're going to be moving in about thirty minutes. You wait until you see us before you break cover."

"I understand."

O'Neill watched Becker disappear into the forest. He became a black, human shape, then a blob without shape and finally he blended into the background. When he was gone, O'Neill turned his attention back to the river and the camp on the other side of it. Another group of black shapes with little definition. He wasn't going to move until he could see some definition. That would mean the sun was coming up and by the time they crossed the river, it would be bright enough to see well.

Again he glanced at his watch and then up into the night sky. Except that it wasn't night anymore. Now it was early morning. The blaze of stars, so sharp and clear at night, was now fuzzing and fading. The first hints of dawn were spreading up into the sky.

O'Neill climbed to his knees. To his left came a faint snore. Someone had fallen asleep. In a real war, if he had a real army, he could shoot the offender. But this wasn't war and he hadn't told them to stay awake. He wouldn't make that mistake again.

Standing, he pushed a few branches to the side. Now he could see the opposite bank and a few of the mud huts. It was time. He checked his rifle and made sure the safety was off. Wouldn't do to rush into battle with a weapon that wouldn't fire.

He moved forward slowly, stepping carefully. He didn't

want to slip on the wet mud and plunge into the river. Besides looking stupid, it might alert the enemy.

He reached the edge of the water and turned back to look. The rest of his army was slipping from the shadows and moved down to join him. Grinning in spite of himself, O'Neill entered the water. At first he didn't feel a thing but then it reached above his boot tops, soaked through his clothes and poured in. It was tepid. Not chilly, as he had expected, nor hot. Just tepid.

Moving forward, the water reached his knees and crotch and finally to his waist, but no higher. There was pressure from the current but it was slight and easy to defeat. He stepped on something, came up slightly, out of the water, and then stepped down. A log or rock under the surface.

When they reached the far bank, he stopped and glanced at his soldiers. Now they were all in knee-deep water, the faint glow of dawn showing them in stark relief. He crouched, one knee in the water, and stared up, into the camp. There was no movement there and for a moment he was afraid that it was abandoned. He'd look stupid, inept, if it was abandoned.

Without thinking further, he stood again and waved a hand, signaling his army forward. They left the river, climbed the gently sloping bank and found themselves near the village. Again he halted, letting the sun get a little higher and throw a little more light on the subject.

O'Neill was vaguely aware of the other two groups, led by Becker and Jones moving through the river. He was aware of the quiet around him. Only the lapping of the river against its bank. No insects, animals, or birds. It was as if the creatures killed everything near them, maybe for food or maybe for sport.

He decided that it was time. He moved through the knee-high grass and out onto a plain. There was a single structure in front of him. Mud and thatch with openings for windows but no sign of glass in them. The door was a curtain of grass woven into a pattern. O'Neill didn't care. He wanted the assault to begin. He centered himself in front of it, took a grenade from his belt, armed it, and tossed it into the hut. Then, leaping to the side, he waited.

An instant later there was a flat bang and the thatch burst into flame. A scream came from inside the hut. Ignoring that, O'Neill screamed, "Get them! Kill them! Kill them all!"

Firing erupted around him as the men and few women began to shoot. Rounds were directed into one hut. They tore at the soft walls, ripping them apart. One collapsed, and part of the roof fell into a swirling cloud of dust. Something stirred from the inside. It staggered into view and was cut down immediately.

"There goes one," yelled a man, pointing at a fleeing figure. "Kill him. Kill him."

A woman's voice sounded. "I got one. I got one!"

Now the sun was higher, the ground brighter. O'Neill could see his people as they infiltrated the three sides of the camp. Fires were breaking out as grenades detonated, the loud, sudden bangs punctuating the staccato bursts of the rifles and shotguns.

He moved deeper into the camp, following one of the mud streets. Two creatures ran from a hut. One of them appeared to be on fire. The second, shorter, one was screaming something unintelligible. O'Neill raised his weapon, aimed at the smaller one, and fired. The force of the round lifted it from its feet and threw it down. It rolled twice and didn't move.

O'Neill didn't shoot at the other. It was on fire. No reason to put it out of its misery. Let it go. He turned and faced another hut. Nothing was moving in it and he knew, just knew, that something was hiding inside. He took a step toward it and the door seemed to explode outward. There were three of them, waving clubs and screaming. No warning. Just a sudden attack. Just like those made on the defenseless farmers.

O'Neill, however, wasn't defenseless. He slipped to one knee, aimed, and fired. The first of the creatures was spun to the right. It lost the grip on its club as it fell to the ground.

Behind him were more shots. A wild burst of them, and the last two beasts fell under a hail of bullets. One tried to rise, was hit again and again, and then collapsed to the ground.

O'Neill pushed through the camp, to the other side of it. He stopped near a low mud wall, crouched and turned to watch. He lifted his rifle, searching for a target but found none in the flickering firelight.

Around him, his men swarmed, screaming their hatred. A big man chased a small creature, swinging at it with the butt of his rifle. He finally knocked it from its feet. It rolled to its back and began to wail like a kid attacked by an adult. It kicked and flailed its arms, but that didn't stop the man. He stood over it, screaming obscenities as he raised his weapon high to smash downward.

A mother ran from a flaming hut, its baby cradled in its arms. One man fired at it, missed, and fired again, missing again. A second man pushed the first aside and fired. He hit the mother, knocking her from her feet. She tried to get up, to protect her baby, but was too badly wounded.

"I'll get it," shouted the man. "I'll get it." He aimed at the child and killed it.

O'Neill stood up and watched as his army searched the huts, dragging the rudimentary furniture and personal possessions out. The men destroyed what they could and tossed the rest into the fires.

The shooting began to taper off. O'Neill figured they had killed all of the enemy. He lifted a hand to his mouth and ordered, "Cease fire!"

But as he did, a half dozen creatures burst from cover, running for the protection of the river. They dodged among Becker's men and women. One of them raised a powerful fist and slammed it down, onto the shoulder of a man. The man collapsed, shrieking in sudden pain.

"Get them!" yelled Becker. He opened fire again.

"Stop them," shouted a man. "Kill them."

O'Neill leaped the short mud wall and sprinted forward. He joined Becker, firing at the fleeing beasts. One fell, sprawling forward on its face. A second was hit, stumbled on, and then dropped. The third and fourth went down, and finally the fifth was killed. But the sixth leaped, stretching out like a swimmer at the beginning of a race. It hit the water, slipped from sight for a few moments. The water where it disappeared churned under the impact of the bullets.

"We've got to kill it," shouted O'Neill. He charged down to the river's edge. He began to wade in, saw the creature's head reappear as it took a deep breath. O'Neill fired from the hip. The bullet struck the water with a splash. The creature disappeared and O'Neill knew that he had missed it.

Becker joined him, the breath rasping in his throat. "Where'd it go?"

"Don't know," said O'Neill. He turned up river, watching the surface of the water, searching for a sign.

"We'll get it," said Becker.

"Doesn't matter any more," said O'Neill. He laughed. "Who's it going tell? The colonial office? Forget it." He turned and walked back up the bank.

A man ran up to him. He carried the head of a dead creature by the hair. He grinned, wiped the sweat from his face in what might have been a partial salute and reported. "I think we got them all."

"Except the one in the river."

"Hell, Cap'n, who gives a fuck if one got away." He glanced at the head he held and then displayed it for O'Neill. "Got this one."

"That you did."

Pruggs appeared then, walking between two smashed huts, stepping over the bodies of the creatures killed. He stopped short and said, "Maybe a half dozen came at us. Cut them down. I've brought my boys in. No sense in staying out there in the grass."

"Good. Let's get the rest of the people collected and get back across the river."

"We lose anyone?" asked Pruggs.

"Hell, I don't know. We'll find out soon enough, won't we?" said O'Neill.

O'Neill walked toward the river again. He didn't bother to look back at the destruction. He didn't care about it. The enemy had been there and he was interested in killing it. Eradicating it.

Becker caught him near the edge of the water. "That'll put the fear of God into these heathens."

Now O'Neill couldn't help himself. He began to laugh. He threw his head back and roared. Finally he glanced at Becker and said, "I wanted to put the fear of us into them. To hell with God. Make them afraid of us."

"Yes, sir," said Becker. He understood that completely.

7

ON THE SS *CLIFFORD McKLUSKY*

JOHN, SIX ONE TWO, stood in the observation port and stared out into the blackness of space. There was a blaze of brightness that marked the galactic center and a distant disc that was the star closest to the ship. He could see no planets near the star.

A voice behind him said, "An impressive sight."

John, Six One Two, turned. The female lieutenant who had shown him everything she had was standing there. This time she was in full uniform.

"Yes," he said.

"I hope that it wasn't something I did that made you change your cabin assignment."

He turned his attention back to space. He didn't like the way she stared at him. He was embarrassed by the incident. He was embarrassed by her actions and his reactions and wished that she would just go away.

"I didn't mean anything by it," she said. "It's just that I still have a hard time accepting the co-ed facilities. I sometimes think that our drive to prove that everything is equal opportunity has taken things too far."

John, Six One Two, didn't fully understand what she was talking about. He and his brothers and sisters had always shared the facilities. No one thought twice about it. He knew that his sisters were different than he was, that their bodies were different than his, but he'd never thought much about it. It was the difference between boys and girls and didn't mean much of anything.

"My name's Lisabeth Conners."

He glanced over his shoulder. "John," he said. He almost added, Six One Two, but had been told not to use the numbers with outsiders. They wouldn't understand.

Conners moved closer to him. He felt her breath on his neck and didn't like it. She was standing too close to him. Much too close. He wanted to say something to her, wanted to force her to move away, but knew that it wasn't the polite thing to do. He'd been told that a number of times.

"I hope that you'll forgive me," she said, her voice low, husky.

John, Six One Two, felt himself react to her proximity and to her voice and didn't like it. He wanted to get away from her. He slipped to the right, turned, and pushed to the rear so that she was now in front of the observation port.

"Beautiful, isn't it?" she said. "Makes you think."

"I have duties," he said suddenly. "Important duties. I must go."

He nearly leaped into the corridor. He hurried down it, refusing to look back, afraid that Conners would be following him. He reached the mid-lift, got in, and headed down to where the rest of the platoon waited.

The platoon's bay was empty, which was exactly what he had expected. They were in training, simulating an assault on a primitive village. A search and secure mission that he should be watching. Sara, Six One Three, was in tactical command, giving her an opportunity to run the platoon in case he was killed or wounded and unable to command.

For a moment he stood at the hatch, looking at the bay itself. Standard military issue. A small room, cargo compartment, storage facility no more than forty feet long and sixteen feet high. The individual cubes, six feet by three feet by three feet, made up the private space. Each of his brothers or sisters was assigned a cube in which to sleep or rest or relax. There were nearly opaque screens for privacy, but since they were the enlisted troops, no one trusted them.

But still, they were not isolated as he was. He had the

privilege of a private room, he had the privilege of eating in the officers' mess on four place plastic tables covered with a synthetic cloth. He wasn't required to bathe or excrete in front of a dozen others, or sleep in a cabin with forty others.

And standing there, looking at the bay, he wished that he could. They had friends in the platoon. Some of them were close to the others while all he had was a working relationship with his oldest sister, a less-important relationship with his brothers and sisters assigned as squad leaders, and almost no relationship with any of the others. He was all alone at the top of the pyramid and he didn't like it there.

Finally he turned and walked down the corridor, found the mid-lift and stepped on. He rose, or descended, or whatever, through the center of the ship and stopped on a deck near the outer hull.

This was the training area, an open deck that could be configured to allow a different training problem each twenty-four-hour period. His platoon was there, at the far end, assaulting the enemy village.

Before he could step away from the mid-lift, an inspector appeared. "How my I help you, Lieutenant?"

"That's my platoon. Over there."

"Yes, sir. How may I help you?" she asked again.

John, Six One Two, looked at the woman. Small, almost tiny. Dark hair and dark features. Quite different from his sisters. He shrugged at her and said, "I wanted to watch."

"Certainly sir. Please follow me to the umpire's shack."

She turned and moved off, through the brightly colored vegetation. Yellows, oranges, and violets so vivid that they hurt the eyes to look at them.

"This what the world we're going to looks like?" he asked.

Glancing over her shoulder, she said, "We have no way of knowing since we don't know what your assignment is going to be once you're attached to the infantry. This happens to be a representation of the vegetation of Epsilon Eridani."

"Oh."

She kept walking, turned, and entered what seemed to be the trunk of a gigantic red tree. The door shimmered about a foot off the ground.

Inside was a communications center complete with two dozen vid-screens and three holotanks. The umpires, two men and a woman, sat at the console watching as the platoon worked its way through the mud huts and the mechanical targets.

He watched as two of the platoon members ran across an open area, dove at the door of a hut, and disappeared inside. An instant later the roof of the hut fell in on them with a burst of smoke and dust.

"Warned them about booby traps," said one of the umpires.

"They weren't hurt were they?" asked John, Six One Two.

"Nope. They're dead for the rest of the exercise and their skin will burn with a slightly maddening itch for the next forty-eight hours, but they weren't hurt."

"Why the itch?"

"A reminder of their stupidity," said the umpire.

Sara, Six One Three, appeared in the center of the village. She stood with her laser rifle clutched in her left hand. There was dirt smeared on her face and across her back.

"I think it's time to throw a little cold water on the exercise," said the woman umpire. She reached across the console, touched a button and then sat back, a self-satisfied grin on her face.

"What?" asked John, Six One Two.

"Just wait and see."

There was a roar, first low, barely audible. It built slowly, like a freight train that was just beginning to roll. Low, quiet, rumbling. Sara, Six One Three, turned toward the right and stared at the vegetation outside the village.

Two soldiers emerged from a hut and ran toward her, stopping short. Their attention was drawn off toward the sound. Their voices came through the speakers.

"What the hell?"

"Where's second squad?"

"Deployed there, at the edge of the village." One man lifted a hand and pointed.

Another man appeared, his weapon held in both hands. He stood flat-footed, staring into the vegetation. "We've got to do something about that."

"What?"

"Form the platoon there to meet the threat."

John, Six One Two, immediately realized the flaw in their thinking. No threat had appeared. Just a roaring that could be interpreted as a number of things, including a natural phenomenon that they didn't understand.

Sara, Six One Three, nodded and turned. "I want third squad up here now."

A half dozen people swarmed from the far end of the village, running toward her. She asked, "Where the hell are the rest of the people?"

"Dead."

"We haven't seen a single enemy soldier and we're taking casualties?"

There was no response to that. One of the men looked around wildly. "It's getting closer."

The roar was increasing in intensity. Now the platoon had to shout to be heard over the noise. More of them appeared from their defensive positions. They stood in a ragged line facing the roaring.

"Gets them every time," said one of the umpires. "Let's key the enemy counterattack now."

The woman touched another button and John, Six One Two, watched as enemy soldiers poured out of the vegetation on the side of the village opposite the roaring. No one in the squad saw them coming or sensed them attacking.

The assault force stopped short, aimed their weapons, and then one of the attackers commanded, "Surrender. Or die."

Sara, Six One Three, whirled, her weapon aimed. A weak laser flashed out, touched her chest, and she was no longer a part of the exercise.

One or two others made sudden moves and were burned down too. The others surrendered quickly and the exercise ended. The platoon had been eliminated without inflicting a single casualty on the enemy. They had destroyed a couple of mud huts, found no weapons, and done no damage to the enemy's war-making capabilities.

"You see what they did wrong?" asked one of the umpires.

John, Six One Two, nodded. He understood it completely. They had entered the village because it was there, had let their attention be diverted, failed to establish and maintain proper security, and then had bunched up at the end.

"Your sergeant seems to lack the proper training to command. That is a mistake on your part."

"Our training has been conducted by others," said John, Six One Two. "I've had no hand in it."

"You should have said something."

"Training was not my responsibility. It's not my fault."

"Well, your platoon was eliminated in little more than an hour in the simulator. I hope that they function better under your command and that you don't get killed."

"I am not the one being scored here," said John, Six One Two, his voice rising in anger. "I was not tasked with this activity."

The umpire shrugged. "Just trying to let you know what our report will say."

"You're not being fair. You don't know what I can do, yet you're going to blame me. That's not fair."

"We call them as we see them. Your platoon does not function well under combat conditions . . ."

"This was not combat. It was a stupid exercise designed to make me and my platoon look bad."

The umpire turned in his seat and stared up at John, Six One Two. He was going to respond and then shook his head. He let his attention return to the screens in front of him.

John, Six One Two, exited the umpire's shack. He stood near the mid-lift waiting for his platoon. They walked out of the vegetation a moment later looking dejected, like a Little League team that had lost their first game by a one-sided score.

Sara, Six One Three, spotted the lieutenant and moved toward him. She carried her rifle in her left hand and clutched her helmet by the chin strap in her right. "They didn't play fair," she said.

"I know."

"Made me look dumb. I don't like that."

"I told them that," said John, Six One Two. He moved closer to the mid-lift.

The woman umpire came from the shack and said, "The two of you are to report to the training officer, Colonel Hartford, before you quit for the day."

"Great," said John, Six One Two. "It's getting close to time for dinner."

"The colonel is waiting."

"So?" asked John, Six One Two.

"Well, I wouldn't want to be the one who kept him waiting. I'd advise you to see him first. Before you eat."

"Oh, all right," snapped John, Six One Two.

The mid-lift arrived and the platoon climbed into it. As soon as the doors shut, they exploded into noise, complaining about the unfairness of the exercise, that they had been scared for no good reason, that the umpires were unfair and cheated, and that they couldn't see a reason to play these stupid games.

John, Six One Two, held up his hands, as he'd seen others do, and waited, but they kept shouting at him. Finally he yelled back. "Shut up. Shut up. Shut up. Shut up."

One by one his brothers and sisters fell silent. One or two of them looked at him, resentment marking their faces. It was obvious they were thinking that he wasn't that much older, and they knew he wasn't any smarter.

"Now," said John, Six One Two, "let's act like men and women here. You get back to your area and clean up, get ready for dinner. Timothy, Seven, One One, will be in charge until we get back."

Someone mumbled something. John, Six One Two, stared into their faces and asked, "What was that?"

No one responded.

"That's what I thought too." He surveyed them all slowly, waiting for someone else to say something back, but they were all now silent.

The mid-lift slowed and stopped. John, Six One Two, and Sara, Six One Three, stepped aside and let the rest of the platoon out. Once the were gone, the doors shut and they began the sideways slide through the center of the ship that would take them to the command deck.

A moment later the mid-lift stopped and the doors opened. John, Six One Two, stepped out, waited for Sara, Six One Three, and together they walked down the corridor.

The command deck was different than the rest of the ship. There were no guards on duty, and the beams, pipes, and wires that lined the lower corridors were either missing or routed through the bulkheads to conceal them. The paint on the bulkheads was of deeper colors, blues and greens and browns. Carpeting covered the deck, and the lighting overhead was bright but pleasant.

"We should live this way," said John, Six One Two.

"We will," said Sara, Six One Three. "Very soon we'll be up here."

A young lieutenant met them outside the hatchway that led into Colonel Hartford's office. They were told to sit, and the lieutenant announced them to the colonel.

Hartford appeared a moment later, gestured at them so that they remained seated, and then dropped into the single chair opposite them. He saw the looks on their faces and asked, "First time here?"

"Yes, sir," said John, Six One Two.

"It can be impressive. We like to pretend that we deserve the luxury because of our sacrifices as we climbed the ladder, and that rank does have it's privileges. I believe that an officer should only avail himself of those privileges if it is in connection with his function."

"Sir?" said John, Six One Two.

"I suggest," said Hartford, "that the colonel not move to the front of the line unless he has a legitimate reason for doing so. If there is no pressing work, a staff meeting coming up, or a deployment, then he should wait in line just as all the enlisted personnel, NCOs, and junior officers are required to do."

"Yes, sir," said John, Six One Two.

"Yes, well," said Hartford. "I didn't summon you here to treat you to the theories of Colonel Hartford. We are approaching your destination."

"The navigator told me that we wouldn't be near a planet for more than two weeks," said Sara, Six One Three.

Hartford grinned and said, "You've got me there. However, we are close to your destination. We're rendezvousing with a fleet. You'll be transferred to the fleet."

John, Six One Two, nodded. "Yes, sir."

"You seem to show a lack of curiosity about your assignment."

"Yes, sir."

Hartford stood up and walked toward the bulkhead where a map of one section of the galaxy had been hung. He seemed to study it for a moment and then turned. "If there are no questions, then you're free to go."

"Yes, sir."

"Lieutenant. Have your platoon ready for deployment in the morning. Weapons are not to be loaded, grenades are to be stored and safed. No other explosives, sonic mines, or anti-personnel gear will be taken. Understood?"

"Yes, sir."

"I'll have Lieutenant Rydell escort you to the mid-lift."

"Yes, sir."

Hartfort left the cabin and Rydell appeared. "If you'll follow me."

"That seemed like a waste of time," said John, Six One Two. "An order would have taken care of the problem."

"The colonel believes in telling the troops about their orders to their faces when possible."

They reached the mid-lift. The doors opened. As they did, Rydell said, "You'll have your orders in the next four hours. Please be ready for them."

Both John, Six One Two, and Sara, Six One Three, entered the elevator. The doors closed quietly and as they did, John, Six One Two, slammed a hand against the wall with a quiet thud. "Those dummies treat us like we're kids. Like we can't find our way without their help."

"I don't think they mean it," said Sara, Six One three.

"You don't know, either," he snapped. "You don't know anything either."

They rode back to the platoon area in silence.

8

FLAGSHIP OF THE TENTH INTERPLANETARY INFANTRY REGIMENT

JEFFERSON SAT IN his cabin, at the tiny desk with the computer keyboard, VTD, and the link into the ship's mainframe. He was periodically typing in information, watching as the computer searched for the correlations, errors, and errata. He had some ideas, but none of them were doing him any good.

The chime at the hatch sounded and he touched a button, clearing the screen. Torrence stood there, looking up at the camera, waiting for him to recognize her and open the hatch. Instead he said quietly, "It's open."

Torrence entered, crossed to his bunk and sat down on the edge of it.

Turning to face her, he asked. "You have something on your mind, Vicky?"

"Update on our long lost platoon. They'll be joining us at noon."

"Damn. You learn anything new about them?"

"They've got the ear of the general. Or rather, his interest. We've got to provide weekly reports to him, telling him everything that is going on."

Jefferson was going to complain about it, to tell her that he didn't like it, but it had all been said before. There was nothing new to be added. He could bitch about it and Torrence would nod and agree, but the platoon would still show up and they would still have to provide the reports.

"You ready to deploy?"

"Once we're near the planet, I can be on the ground within two hours, depending on how you want to handle it."

"This isn't one where we have to hide the technology. It's a colony planet with low-grade primitives on it. Use the shuttles and the local spaceport."

She grinned. "Yes, sir." She leaned back on her hands for a moment and then twisted around, lifting her feet up, onto the bunk. She stretched out, hands behind her head, looking as if she was resting on a lazy, summer afternoon.

"Comfortable?" asked Jefferson.

"Yes, sir." She snapped out the words as if she was on the parade ground but she didn't move a muscle.

Jefferson shifted around, touched a couple of keys clearing the screen. He exited the files but left the computer running. He stood up and stepped to the bunk so that he could look down at her. Torrence was a good-looking woman. A strong, intelligent woman who could command the regiment as well as he could. Maybe better. She was self-confident and reliable.

"What do you have on your mind?"

"Got most of the regiment involved in a minor training exercise this morning. Two companies are working their way through the arms locker, checking the weapons, power packs, ammunition, and the other equipment. Another company is on the KP circuit preparing for the next month. Martuesi and the last two companies are meeting with intelligence for intensive briefings before deployment."

"What are you telling me?"

"Everyone has something to do. Everyone will be tied-up until the middle of the afternoon. No questions, interruptions, disturbances, or panic decisions." She reached for the top button of her tunic.

Jefferson stood there flat-footed, not moving. He watched her finish her task, letting her tunic fall open, revealing her bare skin from neck to waist. The edges of the tunic just covered her nipples.

The complications loomed in front of him again. It was an on-going struggle. They both were aware of the trouble that their personal relationship could cause, but both seemed to be ignoring that.

She reached for her belt buckle, fumbled with it, and then unbuttoned and unzipped her uniform trousers. She lifted her hips and slip them down to her knees. "You'll have to help now."

Jefferson thought of all the arguments against it, as he always did, and felt himself failing again. He was looking at the soft skin of her thighs and at the thin fabric that barely covered her.

It was then that the door chime sounded again. He turned and glanced at the screen. One of the sailors stood there, looking up at the camera, waiting.

"Great timing," said Torrence. She made no effort to dress. "I spent three hours arranging it so that there'll be no one around to bother us and Captain Clemens takes care of it."

Jefferson laughed and thought, saved by the bell. To Torrence, he said, "Captain Clemens wouldn't send one of his sailors if it wasn't important."

"We've got computers, intercoms, interphones, and a dozen other ways to communicate." Now there was anger in her voice. She still hadn't made a move to dress.

"Vicky?"

"To hell with it. I'm not moving."

Jefferson shrugged. He opened the hatch and then stood so that the sailor wouldn't be able to see Torrence.

The sailor saluted and said, "Captain Clemens' compliments, sir. He wished to inform you that the rendezvous will be early. The SS *Clifford McKlusky* is within easy hailing range and transfer of the platoon will commence within the hour."

"Thank you, sailor."

"Yes, sir. My pleasure." He saluted again and disappeared.

Jefferson closed the hatch to find Torrence standing up. Her trousers were now around her ankles.

"Not very dignified," he said.

"Just wanted you to get the best view." She swung her tunic open and stood with her hands on her hips. After a couple of seconds, she said, "That's all you get." She bent at the waist and pulled up her trousers.

"You'll join us in the shuttle bay?"

"Hell, I wouldn't miss it."

• • •

O'Neill led the column of ATVs into the town. He stood in the rear, holding onto the roll bar like a general in the back of a jeep inspecting his troops. There were only a few colonists on the streets. No one had announced the big victory so only those who were in the town knew about it.

But the word spread fast, and as they reached the outskirts to turn and head back again, more people arrived. Now there were cheering men, women, and children lining up to watch the impromptu parade.

Glancing over his shoulder, at the short line of vehicles, he could see more of his men standing as he did. One of them held the severed head of a local up, displaying it for the cheering mass. Others held bloody clubs and one of the ATVs had the body of a local tied over the fender.

They drove through the town again and then O'Neill pointed at the colonial headquarters. "Pull in there," he said. "Let's show Nast what we've done."

The driver did as he was told. The other vehicles did the same, lining up side by side. O'Neill hopped out of the back and then turned, looking at his makeshift army. He knew they'd want to hear some encouraging words from their captain.

He waited for them to line up close to their vehicles. The civilians moved forward slowly, almost surrounding the soldiers. They were mumbling quietly, the cheering having died out.

O'Neill wiped a hand over his forehead. He looked at the sweat there, surprised because it didn't seem to be so hot. He glanced up at the sun and then back at his soldiers.

"Men, we went in harm's way. We searched for the criminals who had attacked our fellows and killed them. We have extracted retribution for it, but we're not finished. The job is a long way from finished."

There was a moment's silence and then the cheering began. The men were shouting, waving the trophies they had taken in the attack. The severed heads and arms and legs were raised high for all to see. The crowd that had filtered in behind them started a chant, first only a few but then all of them, screaming their approval.

Nast burst from the colonial office. He stood, the sun

shining in his face, staring up at O'Neill. He waited for the cheering to die out and then said, his voice tinged with anger, "I said I didn't want a massacre."

"No massacre, Mister Nast," spat O'Neill. "Retribution." He was silent for a moment and then gestured at the assembled crowd who had begun cheering again. Over that noise, he shouted, "They approve and that's all that we care about."

Nast surveyed the crowd slowly, a hand up to shade his eyes. Finally he looked up at O'Neill. "I want to see you in my office."

"You'll have to wait until the parade is over."

"No, sir, I do not have to wait. You get in there now with your top lieutenant."

"Then you'd better smile or the crowd will riot. They all approve."

Nast turned suddenly and disappeared. As the door closed, O'Neill lifted his hands, calling for silence. When he had it, he announced, "Ladies. Gentlemen. My colleagues and I have been invited to meet with the colonial director." He searched the crowd and spotted Becker. He pointed and said, "Nast wants to see the both of us."

Becker moved forward through the crowd, and asked, "We in trouble?"

"Nah. Nast thinks so but look at the people around us. He tries anything and they'll lynch him."

O'Neill pushed his way through the crowd. People were pounding him on the back and grabbing at his hand to shake it. Their words filled his ears. Congratulations. Thanks. A job well done. He grinned at them, nodded at them, but kept on moving toward the door.

As soon as he and Becker had made it through, Nast shouted, "Just what in the hell did you do?"

"We discovered an armed force of those creatures and we attacked it. We eliminated a force, maybe the force that was raiding our farms."

Nast seemed to deflate. He stepped to the rear and sat on the desk there. "They were armed?"

"That's right. Forty or fifty of them, and we killed them all. No reason to let any of them survive. You find a rogue cat, or a pack of wolves, you kill them all."

"You're sure they're the ones who've been attacking our farms?"

"They might not have been involved in all the attacks," said O'Neill, "but you can bet the ranch they committed some of them."

"All right," said Nast. "I just don't like seeing people celebrating the deaths of others."

"Hell, they're celebrating the release from fear. With us retaliating against the creatures, they know that there will be fewer attacks. That's what they're celebrating."

"I suppose you're right."

Becker spoke up for the first time. "You know what would be good? You, Mister Nast, and us, me and Dick, and a couple of the others on stage, with the rest of the command in the rear. A meeting with the population. Tell them about the attack. Tell them about the fight. Let them know what happened when we hit the enemy."

"Yeah," said O'Neill. "I like that. Tell them what happened and what they can now expect."

"I don't like it," said Nast.

"You wouldn't because you weren't there, but if you'd gone in harm's way with my boys and girls, you'd want to celebrate too. Those who sit back at home, safe, while their fellows are fighting for their freedom and protection, always want to minimize the glory gained. They didn't participate, so they think that anything done for those who did is overdone. My boys and girls deserve a celebration, broadcast over the colonial cable so those living far away can see what's happening."

Nast rubbed his chin in thought. "I'm afraid it would inspire others to go hunting."

"Not hunting," said O'Neill. "Defending." His voice took on added confidence as he spoke. He knew that, at that moment, he controlled the colony. Anything he said to the people would be believed. Any orders he gave would be obeyed.

"Besides, a few more expeditions wouldn't hurt. Punitive expeditions against these creatures to teach them a lesson."

"The military is getting close," said Nast.

"What? You want to turn government over to a bunch of soldier boys and girls?" asked O'Neill. "I thought you wanted to take care of the problem by yourself. Be the hero of the colonial office because you solved the problem."

Nast stood up and walked around the desk. He sat down in the chair, propped his elbows on it, and then folded his hands. After a moment, he said, "I don't want the entire planet taking up arms. We'd end up with vigilantes running around and it wouldn't be long before the fighting escalated into human against human. I don't want the planet turned into an armed camp."

"We have a problem and we're taking steps to eliminate it," said O'Neill. "That's all we're doing. But if you're concerned, I suggest that you officially appoint us as the only militia. All others will be forced to disband."

"I don't like creating an army," said Nast.

"It's not an army. Not a professional army. It's us. Farmers who have fields to attend later." He glanced back at Becker. "But let me say this. You don't appoint us officially, we'll still be organized and the people will support us. You won't be able to do a thing about us."

Nast sat quietly for a moment. Finally he nodded and said, "I'll make the announcement tonight when we hold the celebration in the town hall. Complete, planetwide broadcast for as long as you want. Preemption of all other programming, plus recording and packaging of tapes to be sent to each farmstead."

"All right!" shouted Becker.

"Uniforms," said O'Neill.

"Design them and we'll get them made."

O'Neill was feeling his power. He moved forward and sat on the edge of the desk. Nast recoiled at the odor of a man who'd been in the field without benefit of clean clothes or a bath. O'Neill grinned and said, "Weapons. These hunting rifles are inadequate for our purposes here. We should have laser weapons, pistols, and grenades. Maybe a field piece or two."

"There's no need for artillery," said Nast.

"How can you know? Two weeks ago there was no need for an armed militia. It's better that we be prepared for anything than wish we had thought ahead."

"If things get out of hand," said Nast, "we can call on the military."

"When did you transmit your call for assistance?" asked O'Neill.

"Two or three weeks ago."

"And they're not here yet. A hell of a lot of us could get dead in that time."

Nast nodded but said, "I didn't suggest that it was urgent they get here. They could respond faster if the need was there."

"We'll be ready, here on Delta Royal Three, in case it takes them too long to get here. You got to remember, we're on our own here. Self-reliant. Can't count on anyone but ourselves."

"All right, O'Neill, you've made your point. But remember one thing. Power is a fleeting commodity. You have it now. A great deal of it now. But one blunder and you'll find the people turning against you. They'll want your scalp, so be very careful."

Looking at Becker, O'Neill said, "I think we've discussed everything we need to talk about. Jason, you have anything?"

"Swords. I think we should have ceremonial swords for our dress uniforms."

"You heard him," said O'Neill.

"Don't push your luck, O'Neill. The real army will be here soon."

"And gone soon. Remember that Nast."

9

ABOARD THE SS *CLIFFORD McKLUSKY*

THE PLATOON WAS lined up in the shuttle bay looking as if they were about to participate in a full-dress parade. They wore their finest uniforms, had their personal equipment polished so that the overhead lights reflected from it, and were standing in four ranks at attention. John, Six One Two, stood in front of them and Sara, Six One Three, stood at the rear and to the right of them. A perfect platoon formation.

It was typical of the army. Hurry up and wait. John, Six One Two, had heard that for all of his short, military career. They had rushed to get to the shuttle bay, had formed up, and then stood under the hot lights waiting for someone to arrive to either tell them something, announce something, or provide them with orders to join the Tenth Interplanetary Infantry Regiment.

The hatch opened and John, Six One Two, turned his head to watch. It irised slowly and Colonel Hartford stepped through, followed by a small contingent of officers. All wore khaki uniforms complete with awards and decorations and highly polished badges of rank.

Hartford crossed the metal deck, the leather of his shoes ringing on the metal. He stopped directly in front of John, Six One Two, and returned the salute. "Have your people stand at ease."

John, Six One Two, raised his voice, turned his head slightly, and ordered, "Platoon! At ease."

Hartford stood in front of them for an instant, staring at them. Finally he began to speak. It was the standard military speech about the coming adventure and how lucky they were to be joining the finest regiment in the universe. He took a moment and explained that Colonel David Steven Jefferson, their new commanding officer, was one of the few living recipients of the Galactic Silver Star, the highest decoration for valor that could be given. They didn't just hand those out like candy to kids. They had to be earned, and it was why Jefferson had climbed so far so fast.

He spoke for twenty minutes, his voice echoing in the metal shuttle bay. Finally he ran down, told them to make themselves proud, and then told them he was proud of them. They'd undergone the strictest training of any unit ever fielded.

When he finished, he handed a packet of orders to John, Six One Two. He saluted, turned, and with his entourage, left the shuttle. As he disappeared through the hatch, John, Six One Two, turned, looked at his platoon and said, "Platoon. Ah-ten-SHUN!"

They snapped to attention. John, Six One Two, said, "Squad leaders, take charge of your squads and move them into the shuttle."

As he turned away, the squad leaders were issuing their orders. Sara, Six One Three, appeared from the rear of the formation. "That was useless."

"Quite. But the brass has to have its day in the sun." He glanced at the packet he held. He lifted it, touched the bottom of it, and saw information appear on the small screen. It was little more than typical orders assigning them all as a special unit to be attached to the Tenth Infantry.

Checking the time, John, Six One Two, said, "We don't have a lot of spare time. Get the troops loaded. I'll wait here."

"Yes, sir."

She turned and hurried off, watching as the squads entered the shuttle. It was a slow process, because each of them carried so much of their own equipment.

John, Six One Two, stood there for a moment, wondering what he should do. It didn't seem right to stand there, in the middle of the shuttle bay, but then, he couldn't get into the control booth at the far end, there were no observations ports to show him the outside, and the hangar doors were still closed. If they had been open, the air would have escaped, killing him. Nothing to do but stand around and look stupid.

He walked toward the shuttle, around to the front of it, studying it. This was a craft designed for flight in space. No streamlined surfaces, no razor-sharp wings, and no control surfaces to catch the nonexistent atmosphere. It was a rounded, blunt thing, designed for maximum cargo-carrying capacity, with the pilots set up high where they could easily see what was going on in front of them. Once in space, they could rotate the craft for the best view. Tiny holes were spaced around the craft. Jets for guidance. To John, Six One Two, it looked like nothing more than a giant egg peppered with tiny holes.

The ramp near the bottom of it was crowded with his platoon. They were shouting at each other, pushing, trying to get in. John, Six One Two, didn't say anything to them. He'd only slow the process. Let them do it, even with all the bitching about it.

The shuttle crew came from the control booth area. John, Six One Two, recognized the lieutenant that he'd shared the cabin with briefly. She stopped short of the hatch that led to the cockpit.

"Morning," she said smiling.

John, Six One Two, returned the smile and nodded, but didn't speak to her.

She hesitated for a moment and then shrugged. She reached up, inside the hatch, grabbed something, and then hauled herself into the craft, lifting her feet first.

Sara, Six One Three, moved over, watched the lieutenant disappear, and asked, "You know her?"

"No, not really. Spoken to her once or twice."

"Well, everyone and everything is loaded. If you're ready, sir."

John, Six One Two, shot her a glance. "What's with you?"

"Nothing. I just don't like you getting too friendly with outsiders."

"She's a fellow officer to whom I have spoken in the past. Nothing overly friendly there."

"It's important that we stick together," said Sara, Six One Three. "She's an outsider."

"By your definition, I'm an outsider too. All the rest of you are enlisted. NCOs might be separated from the lower ranks, but not the way officers are."

"You're one of us," said Sara, Six One Three.

"I would wish that more of you would remember that more often," said John, Six One Two.

"Certainly," said Sara, Six One Three. She reached up and touched him lightly on the shoulder. It was an affectionate gesture. "We have to remember that we're brothers and sisters."

"We must always remember that," said John, Six One Two.

Together they walked toward the shuttle and up the ramp. The seats were arranged around a center pole, spreading out from there. There was a ladder along the center pole and a catwalk to the seats. The whole arrangement could be removed so that other cargo could be loaded in it.

"I reserved seats for us near the top," said Sara, Six One Three.

"No," said John, Six One Two. "I should sit near the hatch so that I can get out first when we land. Military protocol dictates that."

"Of course. I wasn't thinking."

"You're not an aide but a platoon sergeant. There is a difference."

They found seats and strapped themselves in. As they did, the hatch closed with a quiet whine of the servos. The interior lighting changed subtly as the hatch closed. It was dimmer inside, but not dark. There was a murmur of voices as the rest of the platoon talked among themselves.

A quiet voice seemed to surround them. "Please check your seat harness, making sure that the straps are tight. Prepare for lift-off."

A moment later it seemed that they were moving, but he couldn't be sure. Then, suddenly, like an elevator where the bottom had dropped out, they fell into space, outside the influence of the artificial gravity of the ship. There were nervous giggles from both the men and women. Sara, Six One Three, grabbed John, Six One Two's, hand.

"Sorry. Just nervous."

"No problem."

He thought about it though. It was the first time that anyone had ever touched him like that. As if the mere warmth of his flesh would comfort her. Growing up, the environment had been sterile with the doctors, nurses, technicians, teachers, day-care workers, touching only when necessary. No real affection displayed toward him. Or any of the others, for that matter. They hadn't learned the value of human contact and human relationships, and he wondered if that had to do with the role they now filled. They were designated as soldiers from the earliest moment he could remember. Always they had been soldiers, even as toddlers, barely able to walk, they had been soldiers. No affection for soldiers.

He understood the concept. It had been drilled into him because he had been designated the commander from the moment he was born. The others had been allowed to cuddle in groups periodically. They had been separated in some matter that he didn't understand, but he had always been the one alone. Him and Sara, Six One Three. Separate from the others.

Her grip tightened as the attitude of the shuttle changed. Weight increased as the craft accelerated. She leaned toward him, holding on as if he would save her if anything went wrong. He knew that there was nothing he would be able to do, but the fact she felt the confidence made him feel better himself.

The voice spoke again. "We will be docking in just a few moments."

"Looks like we made it," said John, Six One Two. He felt a sudden rush of affection for his sister. This sister. The one sitting next to him, though each of his other sisters looked just like Sara, Six One Three. Some dyed their hair, and one had a scar she'd received when she fell as a little girl, but each of them was a duplicate of the other.

Yet there were differences in them that outsiders couldn't see. He could tell each of them apart, though someone who didn't know them couldn't. There were subtle differences in temperament, attitude, and even ability.

Gravity slipped around them. John, Six One Two, felt it lightly touch him and then settle on him as they entered the shuttle bay of the new ship.

"Once we're down," he said, "you get the platoon formed. I'll check to see what we're supposed to do and where we'll go from here."

"Yes, sir," she said, but she didn't let go of his hand.

John, Six One Two, was aware of that. Aware of the pressure of her fingers, the sweating of her palm against his. And he didn't want to let go either. That little bit of affection, something that had never been shown him, was suddenly extremely important to him.

The shuttle touched down gently. The servos whined, the lights brightened, and the ramp came down. For an instant, John, Six One Two, sat holding hands with his sister, and then, suddenly, knew that he had to move. The flight had been too short. Everything had been too short.

He let go of her hand, unfastened the harness, and stood up. "Get the platoon organized."

"Yes . . . John," she said.

John, Six One Two, froze, looked at her, but didn't change his expression. Emotions flooded through him. Emotions that he didn't understand. He wanted to hold her against him. He wanted to touch her bare skin. He wanted to stay on the shuttle, with just Sara, Six One Three, and ignore everything else.

He forced himself to turn and walked down the ramp into the brightly lighted shuttle bay. A contingent of officers stood to one side. A color guard stood behind them. As he walked down the ramp, a band began to play. John, Six One Two, searched for them and then decided it had to be canned music.

He reached the bottom of the ramp and turned, marching across the deck. He was acutely aware of the chill in the air. The thinness of it. Had the music not been playing, he might have heard the hiss as the air was pumped back into the shuttle bay, filling it to one full atmosphere.

A colonel in a dress uniform came at him, John, Six One Two, stopped and saluted. He knew immediately who the colonel was. The Galactic Silver Star hung on its rainbow-colored ribbon around his neck. The large, silver star, wrapped in an emerald wreath, dangled from the middle of the ribbon. The star was centered over his chest.

"Sir," said John, Six One Two, "we are reporting as ordered."

Jefferson, wearing his dress uniform and the medal that he believed he didn't deserve, stood with the rest of his command staff, the color guard, and a couple of the ship's officers. The medal had been Torrence's idea. She encouraged him to wear it every chance she got. This time he felt it might be useful. Tell the leader of the special platoon that Colonel David Steven Jefferson knew what the hell he was doing.

They waited outside the shuttle bay, inside the control booth, so that he could watch as the egg-shaped shuttle entered, hovered above the deck, and then settled, the feet springing from the underside of the craft to hold it upright.

As soon as it touched down, Jefferson turned, left the control booth, and stopped at the hatch while the air was forced back into the bay. The red light glowed, flickered, and then turned green, telling him that there was now enough air inside the bay.

"Come on," he said. He hadn't figured out why the command staff had to meet the incoming platoon, but the orders had been issued by the commanding general of the department. Welcome the new platoon when they arrived.

Jefferson stepped through the hatch and then moved to the right. He waited as the others followed and spread out. Torrence arranged them the way she wanted them. Jefferson then moved to a position centered in front of them.

The ramp on the shuttle opened but no one appeared for a couple of minutes. Then a single man appeared. A young man in his dress uniform walked down the ramp and came toward him. Jefferson broke formation, moved toward him, and then stopped, waiting.

The young man saluted and said, "Sir, we are reporting as ordered."

Jefferson returned the salute and said, "Have your people fall out and form at the base of the shuttle."

"Yes, sir." The man saluted again, did an about face, and marched back the way he'd come.

Jefferson returned to his own staff. Before he could turn, Torrence said, "So far so good."

As he turned, the whole platoon began exiting the ship. They came down in groups of five, marching together. They began to form the platoon.

"Good God!" said Torrence. "They all look alike."

Jefferson hadn't noticed that. He looked at the faces. Men or women, it made no difference. If it hadn't been for the fact that both sexes were represented, Jefferson wouldn't have been able to tell any of them apart.

"What the hell?" said someone.

Jefferson turned and looked for Captain Carter, the intelligence officer. He was standing at attention with the regimental staff. "Carter. What the hell?"

Carter shrugged and then said, "Why would I know anything more about them?"

"You're the intelligence officer," said Jefferson.

"Yes, sir, but this isn't an intelligence matter."

Jefferson glanced at the rest of his staff. Winston, the personnel officer, stood to one side. "Winston?"

"No, sir. I don't know anything."

Before Jefferson could speak again, the chief medical officer said, "It could be a result of genetic experimentation. Cloning."

"Both sexes?" said Torrence.

"A very little gene manipulation would do that. Shouldn't change the outward traits so you end up with both male and female."

Jefferson stared for a moment and then turned to watch as the rest of the platoon exited. He had thought that each squad would be different, but every one of them looked the same. A group of perfectly matched individuals that had been cut from the same mold. Jefferson thought of the toy soldiers he'd played with as a kid. Groups of soldiers all looking exactly the same. He never thought he'd see the living equivalent of it.

They formed quickly. The platoon sergeant turned command over to the lieutenant, the man who had come out first. She disappeared around the rear of the formation. The lieutenant stood at attention waiting for something to happen.

No one had planned for this. Now they needed some kind of official welcoming speech. Jefferson called Torrence forward, thought about it, and added his adjutant. The three of them, marching in a triangular formation, headed toward the new platoon.

Jefferson stopped, took the salute, and said, "Prepare your platoon for inspection."

Again the lieutenant saluted, did an about face, and ordered, "Open ranks! March."

The first squad took two steps forward, the second one and the last squad took two to the rear. They dressed right, snapped their arms down, and waited. The officer spun again and said, "Platoon ready for inspection sir."

Jefferson noticed the young officer's eyes never left the medal around his neck. Jefferson ordered, "Follow along with me, please."

"Yes, sir."

Jefferson moved to his left, where the first squad leader stood. He moved down the line quickly, studying the faces and uniforms of the men and women there. He stopped, turned, and faced one of the women. "What's you name?"

"Cynthia, One Four Five."

"Where are you from?"

"Sir?"

"Your hometown. Where you grew up?"

She glanced at the lieutenant but didn't answer. Fear clouded her face.

"Never mind," said Jefferson puzzled. Everyone could name his or her hometown.

They reached the end of the first squad, turned, and walked behind them, looking at the rear of the soldiers. They walked along the second squad and then the third and finally the fourth. Nothing varied except the hair color and the badges of rank on the uniforms. The eyes were the same color and the faces the same shape. One woman had a scar but that did nothing other than mark her as an individual.

They returned to the front of the formation. The lieutenant took his position and waited. Jefferson said, "Have them stand at ease."

When the order was issued, Jefferson raised his voice. "I want to take this opportunity to welcome all of you to the Tenth Interplanetary Infantry Regiment. It is the finest regiment in the army. A unit that you can be proud to have joined. Now, in case you've been worried, your platoon will be integrated into the regiment intact. You will stay together."

He stopped and wondered what more to say. He wished he'd thought it out before he had met with them. "In the next few days, once your orientation has been completed, you'll be deployed with a light battalion to a nearby planet. That will be your first regular assignment."

He came to attention and said, "Lieutenant, call your

platoon to attention. Have them fall out. Lieutenant Norris will assist you in getting settled in your quarters."

"Yes, sir."

Jefferson returned the salute, did an about face. He walked back to the staff, stopping long enough to order Norris to remain behind to assist them in getting settled. Without waiting for a response, Jefferson headed for the hatch.

Torrence caught him there. She stepped through after him and said, "What in the hell is that?"

"God, I don't know. That's the strangest platoon I've ever seen. I want everything you've gotten on them since we learned they were coming."

"Yes, sir."

He looked at her. "Did you know they'd all look alike?"

"No, sir. I was as surprised as you were."

"We'll get some answers," said Jefferson. Thinking about it, he didn't know what they would be, but he would get a few answers.

10

DELTA ROYAL THREE

THE MEETING HALL wasn't a necessary structure. The colonial office's business could be conducted over the vid system, reaching everyone at the same time. But there were those who insisted on being present just as in the past there had been fans who insisted on attending the Olympics or the Super Bowl or the World Series in person. There was something about seeing the event live, in person, that was lost with the transmission of it through the air.

And there were those who, living on a farm far from colonial center, rarely saw anyone except spouses and children, who wanted the opportunity to get into town. The meeting hall provided that escape opportunity and it surprised many that events held there were so well-attended.

O'Neill stood in the wings, hidden from the audience, watching as they filtered in, claiming seats. The noise level grew slowly as the audience began to shout questions at one another.

Nast entered through a side door, walked to O'Neill, and then peeked out at the packed house. "I don't want a riot," he said.

"What's to riot? We just tell them about the victory. Tell them that they have nothing to fear from the locals and then everyone goes home."

"Emotions can be inflamed easily," said Nast. "I don't want that happening."

"We'll do our best," said O'Neill.

A young woman appeared. She wore a headset. As she approached, she cocked her head to one side and lifted a hand, pressing the earphone.

She reached them and said, "Mister Nast, I'll announce you first and then you walk to the podium set on the center of the stage. Lights will come up and you read your statement. Then you, Mister O'Neill . . ."

"Captain O'Neill."

"Captain then. You'll enter the same way and do your thing. We're scheduled for only thirty minutes."

"We could run over that time," said O'Neill.

The woman looked helplessly at Nast. He nodded, saying, "We'll have to play it by ear."

"Yes, sir." She turned and hurried away.

The side door opened again and two of the colonial officials, Starling and Clovers, entered. Neither looked happy. They hurried to Nast, glanced at O'Neill, and then said, "We need to talk to you."

"Now?"

"Yeah. It's important."

"Well?"

"Not here," said Starling. She nodded to the right where there was an empty space wrapped in semidarkness.

The woman with the headphones appeared again. "We've got two minutes. Get ready."

"You'd better not do this until we talk," said Clovers.

"You've got a minute," said Nast.

"Can't do it in a minute." Starling looked nervously at O'Neill.

"There's no time now. Wait for me and we'll discuss it after the meeting."

"It'll be too late then."

"One minute," said the woman. "Mister Nast, please get ready." She moved to a microphone held by a stagehand.

The lights came on for the stage and dimmed in the house. The cameraman crouched in front of the podium, focusing on the logo of the colonial office of Delta Royal Three.

The stage manager pointed at the woman with the headset

and she spoke in a quiet, calm voice. "We interrupt our regular schedule to bring you this Special Report. Colonial Commissioner Thomas Nast."

A spotlight hit the curtains and Nast exited, walking across the stage. He stopped at the podium, looked out at the audience as the scattered applause faded.

Nast looked down, saw that the text he'd prepared earlier was sitting there just as it was supposed to be. "Ladies and gentlemen, as some of you know, during the last few weeks a number of attacks have been made against our farms. Evidence has shown the locals responsible for those attacks. A punitive expedition was mounted against the locals responsible. Tonight I am able to report that those responsible have been punished. Tonight everyone can sleep a little sounder, safe in the knowledge that they won't be murdered in their beds."

There was scattered applause, as if the audience wasn't sure if they should clap. But the noise continued building until it was wild cheering. Nast waited for it to subside.

"Tonight," he said, "we have with us the leader of that expedition, Captain Richard O'Neill, commander of our own militia, organized by him for the purpose of protecting all of us. Captain O'Neill and his men are responsible for the peace that has descended over us tonight."

Nast glanced to the wings, saw O'Neill there. "There are many things that I could say here, but this is not the time for them. You want to see Captain O'Neill and hear his story. So, I'll gracefully leave the stage to Captain O'Neill." He lifted a hand and gestured at the wings. "I give you Captain O'Neill."

O'Neill moved slowly across the stage, savoring the building applause and cheering. He reached the podium as pandemonium broke out. He stood there quietly, as Nast abandoned the stage. He waited until the cheering faded and then leaned forward, lips only inches from the microphone.

"Thank you," he said. "Thank you all. It is my pleasure to have served you."

Slowly the meeting hall fell silent. As it did, O'Neill began to speak softly. Suddenly he was in his element. His formal schooling had ended abruptly and he'd never been educated in public speaking or in crowd manipulation, but he understood it completely. He understood what the crowd wanted to hear and he knew exactly how to deliver it to them.

"I was not alone," he said. "Other good men and women accompanied me. Men and women who understood that sometimes it is necessary to sacrifice comfort and home for the greater good of the community. Men and women who saw a job that needed doing and who went out to do it. There was no hesitation. No whining or asking for compensation. Men and women who thought only of their fellows and what they could do to help."

He stopped and the momentary silence was filled with cheering. O'Neill had the audience in the meeting hall, and probably those at home, in the palm of his hand. He could ask for anything he wanted and a planetwide referendum would get it for him.

"You all know that the locals have attacked and killed for no reason. We had negotiated with them in good faith, only to see that good faith turned against us. We provided them with goods, foods, and services in an attempt to help them move from their primitive society into the modern world. But being backward savages, they took our assistance, our goods, and then sneaked about in the night, killing us."

He looked up, into the light, staring up, almost as if looking to heaven for an answer. The crowd was quiet, caught up in the moment.

"This couldn't be allowed. We have the right, the duty, to defend ourselves. This planet is big enough for all of us. A billion people could be added and not tax the resources available here. Two billion and the local population could triple and no one would be pressed for space. It's a huge planet with many resources. Enough for everyone."

Again he stopped and stared out, into the dimness of the meeting hall. He could see the faces of some of the people in the front rows. Beyond that was nothing except blackness.

"But there are always those who want everything for themselves. Those who sign agreements with no intention of living up those agreements. Those who see us as victims. People to be murdered in our sleep. Murdered with our wives and husbands and children. People to be robbed and exploited."

He let the words sink in and then said, "But we're not like that. We don't roll over when pushed. We don't cower in our beds at night. If we did, if we were that type, we'd never have left Earth."

Cheering erupted then. O'Neill grinned and nodded and then held his hands up until he had silence. "I, along with Jason Becker, proposed that we search out the marauders, take the attack to them, and eliminate them. Commissioner Nast, who had called for military assistance, agreed that we were on our own. That we had to do something because the military had yet to arrive. We took the battle to the enemy."

He hesitated, letting that sink in, and then, his voice rising to a shout, said, "We attacked the enemy and we taught him a lesson he won't soon forget."

Now the hall exploded. Men and women were on their feet screaming their approval. O'Neill stood at the podium, calmly watching the demonstration taking place in front of him. He grinned broadly and waited for them to fall silent.

When he had their attention, he said, "I'd like to introduce some of the heroes of the last few days and have them join me on the stage. The first lieutenant of the militia, Jason Becker." He watched as Becker walked toward him. Before he arrived, O'Neill said, "Second Lieutenant Robert Jones . . . Second Lieutenant Helen Byrd . . . First Sergeant Preston Pruggs."

When they had joined him, forming a line behind him, he said, "These are the leaders. The men and women to whom you owe a debt. But there are others. The enlisted ranks. Men and women with no rank, the privates, who did the work. The men and women who did the fighting, risked their lives, to protect all of you, and I think they should join us here, too."

Slowly the men and women filed out, lining up behind the officers. They all stood at attention, some of them obviously nervous about the attention shown them, some of them proud of their role and the opportunity to be singled out.

O'Neill waved a hand as the last of the men joined the formation. "This is your militia. The men and women who have sworn an oath to protect you from all enemies, foreign, domestic, or indigenous. These are the people to whom the debt is owed."

O'Neill, suddenly the master showman, gestured at the men and women behind him and then slowly moved to the left, toward the wings, leaving the militia standing there in the lights with nothing to distract the audience, either in the meeting hall or watching at home.

Again the cheers, applause, the ovation, was thunderous. The cheering lasted for ten minutes before it began to fade. As it did, O'Neill returned to his place at the podium. He glanced at Nast who had not moved from the wings. Grinning at him, O'Neill said, "But the job is not done. We eliminated a small portion of the enemy close to us but there are other bands of them roaming the planet's surface, searching for the easy and helpless prey. Crops are in and there isn't much for us to do now. Let them grow in the bright sunlight and nuture in the rich soil. There is free time to be had now. Free time that we can put to good use."

He waited for the words to sink in. He saw the look on Nast's face because the commissioner had figured out just what O'Neill was up to. Still grinning, he said, "The men and women of the militia will move among you in a few minutes. If you can find it in your hearts to volunteer, will we be able to field a force of sufficient size to destroy the enemy. You can now join us on this great adventure."

Nast took a step out, onto the stage, but stopped as soon as the cheering erupted again. He stared at O'Neill and then retreated again. O'Neill knew that there was nothing he couldn't do at the moment. He held all the power. Nast might be the appointed and official commissioner but, at the moment, O'Neill was the leader. The people would do everything that he wanted. Nast was powerless.

O'Neill reclaimed the microphone as silence descended again. He said, "Before the militia's recruiters move out, I'd like to have some of the members tell you about the battle we have fought. Lieutenant Becker."

As Becker moved to the podium, O'Neill walked to the wings leaving the men and women of the militia to support Becker. He reached Nast and whispered, "What do you think?"

"That was not the agreement," hissed Nast. "A limited militia to deal with a single problem."

"The problem has not been eliminated. We will search out the others and destroy them."

"It's not necessary," said Nast. "The military is on the way. They are trained . . ."

"When they get here, they'll find we've solved the problem ourselves. I thought that was what you wanted."

Nast shook his head. "I wanted a quiet solution. Not this." He had to raise his voice to be heard over the cheering.

"You check your own figures," said O'Neill. "You see if the people here don't agree with what I say."

Again Nast shook his head. He looked up, staring O'Neill in the eyes. "That's what I'm afraid of."

O'Neill turned and faced the stage. There was no doubt about who held the power.

Carter decided that he had seen enough. It was time to alert someone else about what was happening on Delta Royal Three. It was nice of them to broadcast the meeting planetwide so that Carter, with the Tenth Interplanetary Infantry, could intercept the signals and see what was happening.

Carter looked at his assistant, a young lieutenant who had joined the regiment in the last month. To the lieutenant he said, "I'm going to alert Major Torrence. This is going to blow up in our faces. I want everything recorded and I want a hard-copy transcript as soon as possible."

"Yes, sir."

Carter turned his attention back to the screen of the intelligence section. It was a miniature communications center so that Carter would have access to everything that he needed to do his job. He could monitor the television transmissions of any system the fleet was in. Radio signals could be detected from longer distances. The sensor arrays gave him a good look at the conditions on the surface of any of the planets, and the computer hook-ups into the mainframe provided easy access to the stored knowledge that he might need.

The intell section was a dimly lighted cabin with a bulkhead array of screens and keyboards. The data, from whatever source, could be displayed on any of the screens. There was a big screen, nearly four feet across, in the center of the array.

Carter rocked back in the hard plastic chair, touched a couple of keys, and put the relay from Delta Royal Three on the center screen.

Torrence entered a moment later, glanced at the screen and asked, "What the hell is going on?"

Carter pointed at the screen. "That's someone they're calling

Captain O'Neill. He's led a punitive action against the locals."

"Shit!" said Torrence. "What did they do?"

Carter shrugged and pointed at the screen. "According to what I've seen, they attacked a group of locals who supposedly had been attacking the farmers."

Torrence felt the sweat bead on her face. She pulled out the closest chair and sat down. "What can you tell me about these locals? How high are they on the evolutionary scale?"

Carter turned, reached for a keyboard, thought for a moment and then began to type. He finished and said, "It'll be up in a moment. You want it on the center screen?"

"I don't want to lose anything from the planet."

"It's being recorded so we can review it later."

"Then the center screen."

Carter typed another command and said, "This is what we know. There have been no exo-anthropological data. Everything we have is from the colonial office."

"Then it'll be less than accurate," said Torrence.

Carter shrugged. "Probably as accurate as anything you'd get from the anthropologists. The real problem is that no one has spent any time studying the locals. It would take years, maybe decades, to get a real reading on their capability."

"You consulted with Tyson?"

"No reason to. He hasn't had a chance to study Delta Royal Three."

The information appeared on the center screen complete with a photograph, in color, of one of the locals. Carter pointed and said, "This is part of the survey submitted by the colonial office when they applied for approval to colonize."

"Great," said Torrence.

"Hell, if you know the source, you'll be able to read between the lines. Besides, I don't think they actually felt the need to disguise much of the information."

"Let's have it," said Torrence.

"As you can seen, they're humanoid, standing between five five and six five. Two sexes, male and female, with very few external differences." Carter touched the keyboard and a second picture of the creature appeared. She was the same size as the male, though the features of the simian face were softer. Hair matted the head and shoulders. The chests of both beings were amazingly free of hair. There was a band of hair near the knees and another at the ankles.

Both sexes had broad shoulders, but the females tapered to the waist as did human women. They had hands with opposable thumbs. The chins were heavy and someone had mentioned it had to do with being meat-eaters.

"Societal levels?" said Torrence.

More information appeared. They lived in groups and worked together. They were hunters and gatherers with a hierarchy that ran the villages. They lived in small groups, used some tools, and adapted to the influences of the humans. They now used rifles when they could get them, tried to use the radios and the videos, and had even stolen a few of the ATVs.

"Then what you're saying is that they are our equivalent in intelligence," said Torrence.

"Intelligence is a hard thing to measure. How smart are we as a species? How smart are we as individuals? Just what is intelligence?"

"That doesn't answer the question," said Torrence.

"I think the answer is that these creatures are as smart as we are but they don't have the cultural advancement we have. In other words, if they were left alone they would eventually develop a high level of civilization. We can already see the beginnings of it. Local government, individuals who do not participate in the production of food or the creation of anything useful to the society. Rulers whose job is to govern. The society supports them."

Torrence studied the two photographs on the screen. The creatures looked to be stupid brutes. It was the simian features that suggested the chimpanzee to her. Chimpanzees were intelligent, could perform amazing feats, but they were still animals and not human. She knew that she shouldn't let that color her thinking, but she couldn't think of the locals as intelligent. Not without some more evidence.

"Has any testing been done?" she asked.

"Colonial office has no reason to do it and Delta Royal Three is outside the normal space routes. Be a couple of years before any university spends the money to study the local life there."

Torrence rubbed her forehead, massaging her temples. "You think that raid they're talking about was justified?"

"Of course not. I've been watching that show. It's mob action now. You're going to find yourself at odds with them the moment you land on their planet. That O'Neill is not going to give up his power easily. He's too in love with it and he's recruiting a formidable army."

"That's nothing we can't handle," said Torrence. "Hell, we have the legal authority and once we touch down, their authority will disappear."

"I hope you're right."

She looked at him. "You know something that you're not saying?"

"Just that O'Neill likes the power he has and he will not surrender it easily."

"We can work around that," said Torrence.

"I hope you're right."

11

FLAGSHIP OF THE TENTH INTERPLANETARY
INFANTRY REGIMENT

STEVEN GARVEY SAT in the mess hall with the members of the
new platoon. His camera was set on a tripod and he had
impressed one of the crew to run it, explaining that he
shouldn't shift the scene quickly, should keep the person
talking centered in the frame, and should periodically pull
back, shoot a group shot or scan everyone in the room. That
done, he sat down in one of the molded plastic chairs and
began the interviews with the new platoon. He just couldn't get
over the fact that they were all brothers and sisters.

A woman sat down in the chair closest to Garvey. She
smiled at him nervously, just as the others had done, and then
waited for the first question.

"Your name?" asked Garvey.

"Amy, Seven Four Five."

"Amy," said Garvey, "just what in the hell do those
numbers mean. You've all got them."

"It designates the time that we were . . . born. Seven
forty-five in the evening on January twenty-third. John, Six
One Two, was born at six twelve on the morning of January
twenty-third."

"But you have individual names. Why the continued use of
the numbers?" asked Garvey.

"That is the way we've always done it."

Garvey grinned and said, "Since you were born in the evening, shouldn't you be Amy, Nineteen Four Five?"

"I don't know. We all know whether it was morning or evening, so what difference does it make?"

"Good point," said Garvey. "Now, you say born . . ."

She shrugged but didn't say a word.

"I can see that you're all related . . . would the word clone fit?" asked Garvey.

"That's something we don't discuss among ourselves. Born is the word."

Garvey glanced at her suddenly. There was something in her voice that alerted him. She was sensitive about the subject, though he couldn't understand it. In vitro fertilization had been around for more than a century, and though cloning wasn't the same thing it was certainly a kissing cousin. Maybe on Earth there was some discrimination against the clones, but he'd never heard anything about it. He decided to change the subject.

Before he could speak, Amy, Seven Four Five, said, "I don't like this. It's not fun."

"Just a few minutes more," said Garvey. There was a thought then, something about the way she acted, about the way they all acted, but he didn't know what it was. Something strange.

"Do you have ESP?" he asked suddenly.

"I don't understand."

"Twins sometimes develop their own language or sometimes feel and see things that the other sees and feels. I wondered if you shared a linked communication with your brothers and sisters. Something like ESP?"

"No," she said. "We speak English and don't have ESP."

"What's it like having more than forty brothers and sisters?"

"Just like having one or two," she said.

"Do you ever . . . ah, fool around with . . . sex?" asked Garvey.

"NO! I'm not even sure what you mean."

Except that you answered just a little too fast for that to work, thought Garvey. Maybe that was the thing they all wanted to keep quiet. They were all getting it on with one another. And then he thought about it. If the partner was a clone, wouldn't it be like having sex with yourself? A new form of autoerotism. Self abuse with a partner. And, would you be able to anticipate the needs of the partner quicker and easier?

"Are you finished?" asked Amy, Seven Four Five.

"Sure. You can go. Thanks for your assistance."

As she got up to leave, Garvey wondered why none of them expressed the slightest curiosity about where the interviews would play and when they would be aired. It was like the time he'd interviewed a class in elementary school. Excited by the camera and the fact their classes would let out for an hour or so, but no desire or understanding about seeing themselves on the video.

"So you wish to continue?" asked Sara, Six One Three.

"No, not really. Except I'd like to ask you a few questions since you're the oldest."

"Second oldest."

"Oldest one here," said Garvey. "Please?"

Sara, Six One Three, sat down, looked right into the camera lens as if defying it and asked, "What do you want to know?"

"You're the platoon sergeant based solely on the day that you were . . . born?"

"As the second oldest, I have responsibilities that the others do not."

"At most you're only hours older than the youngest of the brothers and sisters. It can't make that much difference."

"But it does," she said. "I have great responsibilities."

"Even when you were growing up?"

"What do you mean?"

"When you were younger, did you still have greater responsibilities?"

"Of course. I was second oldest."

"Certainly you couldn't have changed diapers or cooked meals."

"Day care took care of that until we were inducted into the military."

"Oh."

"I must go now," said Sara, Six One Three. "We have tasks to perform before lights out."

"Of course," said Garvey, standing. He motioned at the cameraman, a hand knifing across his throat, telling the man to shut the camera off. To Sara, Six One Three, he said, "Thank you, and your brothers and sisters, for their patience with me."

"Of course."

Garvey moved to the camera, collapsed the tripod and lifted it up. He glanced back at the platoon. They were standing around, waiting for him to either tell them to do something or to leave. They didn't seem to care which it was.

To the soldier, he said, "Thanks for the help."

"When's this going to be broadcast?"

Garvey stared at him, wondering if he'd been reading minds. The platoon displayed no curiosity about the broadcast, but the man who ran the camera did. That underscored the difference between that platoon and normal humans.

"I'll try to let you know," he said as he headed out the hatch. As he hurried down the corridor, the thought, normal humans, echoed in his mind. That platoon wasn't quite normal. There was something about them. Something strange, and he didn't think it was all a result of being cloned from the same individual.

That was something he should check. What was the current status of cloning? He knew that the technique had been used to grow donor parts for sick individuals. Cells from the sick person were removed and then used to construct new kidneys, lungs, a heart, or whatever. There wasn't a problem with rejection because the tissues all matched perfectly. He wasn't sure if entire individuals had been cloned . . . He grinned at that. He knew they had been. He'd just seen them. Then how long ago was the first healthy individual cloned? He'd have to get with Carter and see if the intelligence files held anything.

He reached his quarters, entered, and let the automatic lights come up. He pushed the camera into the corner and then turned. There was no way that he was going to remain in his cabin. There was too much going on outside. He would search for someone to give him a couple of answers.

Jefferson sat at the head of the table, a cup of coffee in front of him. A half dozen of his officers, representatives of his staff, and his company commanders were there too, including Courtney Norris, the young woman who was the supply officer. And, of course, John, Six One Two. He was there to be introduced to the regimental staff.

Jefferson had hosted a couple of such meetings to introduce

the new officer to the mess, but this one wasn't going well.
John, Six One Two, seemed to lack some of the social graces
that most officers had learned during their training. A review of
his service record showed that he'd had nearly every course on
small-unit tactics, small-unit management, small-unit rela-
tions, and small-unit capabilities that the army could offer, but
apparently they had overlooked that he would be integrated
into a unit with other officers. He just didn't know how to act
with them.

"Maybe," said Jefferson, "you'd like to share a little of your
background with us.'"

John, Six One Two, got slowly to his feet. He was sweating
heavily though the air-conditioning was working hard. The
mess was small, with a couple of linen-covered tables, molded
plastic chairs, and a service area against one bulkhead that
included a silver tea service. The regimental colors were
displayed there, along with the streamers won on various
battlefields. A holo against one bulkhead gave the impression
that they were looking out into space.

John, Six One Two, wiped a hand over his face and then
rubbed it against his thigh. He looked into the waiting faces of
the other officers, people he didn't know, except for Norris,
who had assisted them earlier, and Jefferson, who was the
commander.

"I've spent the last few years learning the techniques of
commanding a small unit."

"Good," said Jefferson. "Before that?"

"The day care center."

"Schooling?"

"Learned the regular stuff and then entered the special
program designed for me and my brothers and sisters." He
turned toward Jefferson, and then let his eyes slide away
quickly as if afraid to look at anyone.

Jefferson finally took pity on the young lieutenant. It wasn't
that long ago that he'd been a young lieutenant that didn't have
a clue about what he was doing. Jefferson had had a sergeant,
Mason, who had taken him under his wing and taught him. It
was Mason who had crawled out into a rainy, filthy night to
destroy an enemy pillbox that had them pinned down. Mason
should have won the medal that they had hung around
Jefferson's neck. They had promoted him, handed him respon-

sibility, and he had grown into the job. At least he believed he had, and it was the same thing.

"Thank you, Lieutenant," said Jefferson. "Have a seat."

"Colonel," said one of the other officers. "The toast."

Jefferson nodded and stood. He raised his glass as the other members at the table followed suit including John, Six One Two. Jefferson glanced at him but didn't say anything. He said, "To the new platoon and its commander, John Smith."

"To Lieutenant Smith," repeated the officers.

They all drank, including John, Six One Two. Jefferson made a mental note to tell him that he was not supposed to drink when the toast was to him.

As they sat down, Torrence entered. She moved to Jefferson and leaned down, whispering. Jefferson reached up, touched her shoulder and then nodded.

"Ladies and gentlemen, I'm afraid that duty calls. You are encouraged to remain behind and welcome the lieutenant to the regiment. Lieutenant Norris, the duty is yours."

Jefferson stood, saw that the others were about to follow suit, and waved them down. He then followed Torrence out into the corridor. "Now, what in the hell is going on?"

"I've just come from intelligence. Watching the planetary broadcasts. They're going a little nuts down there."

"Communications with Nast indicated that they were handling the problem."

"They have been. That's the problem." She touched her lips with the back of her hand. "They've formed a local militia that has attacked the locals."

"That a problem?"

"Yes, sir, I think it is. The locals may be primitive, but they are an intelligent species. Agreements have been reached with them about our expansion to their planet but apparently there have been incidents."

"Which resulted in our being here."

"I think the situation is a little more serious than Nast and his colonial office have let on."

"Meaning?"

"That militia for one. They've got a captain, probably self-appointed, but they've got a captain who understands mob psychology. He was whipping the human population into a frenzy, and I think we're going to have trouble with them."

Jefferson took a deep breath. "I was afraid of something like this. You sure it's that bad?"

"Colonel, I saw him on the stage and I saw some of his soldiers. They were displaying the heads of the locals killed, holding them up like trophies after a ball game."

"You sure it wasn't justified?"

"Sir, I don't know anything about that situation except that we'd better speed up our schedule. And I'll tell you something else. I can't think of one example where a wholesale slaughter had been justified."

"Anything from Nast?" asked Jefferson.

"No, sir. Routine traffic. He answers our questions but there is nothing to suggest he's anxious for us to arrive."

"I'll get with Carter and review those tapes and then we'll set up a schedule. You done anything with that new platoon?"

"Jesus," she said. "They're a bunch of weird ducks."

"You get anything new on them from headquarters?"

She shrugged. "No, sir. Records are all fine. Nothing irregular about them except that each of them starts seven years ago. Nothing about their lives prior to that. That's a little irregular, but not that unusual.

"I'm afraid that we won't be able to conduct the normal indoctrination training for them if you want to deploy them with our landing force," said Torrence.

"There's not much of a chance of a change. Orders from on high. They're to hit the planet's surface with our forces. You stay close to them until you get a reading on their abilities. Then you can back off or we can recall them."

Torrence leaned against the bulkhead.

"There something else bothering you, Vicky?" asked Jefferson.

"No, sir. I guess not."

"What?"

"Well, sir, it's bad enough we've got to make a planetfall, but I've got to go in with untested troops. I don't like that at all."

"It's a single platoon and it's not as if you're landing in a deadly situation. The problem might have been solved by the colonial office and their militia."

"And it might have been made worse by them. This is not a good situation."

12

DELTA ROYAL THREE

THE PEOPLE WERE lined up outside the meeting hall three abreast. The line stretched down the block. O'Neill couldn't believe that so many humans lived on the planet. More than he would have guessed. And more in this area, where they could get there to sign up for the militia, than he could believe.

And he had Jones on the video signing up recruits from the other areas of the planet. The only deal was they had to arrive in the next two days.

Becker stood at the window, looking out, and said, "I can't believe the response. So many people."

"That's an indication of how much damage has been done by the locals. Everyone has felt the sting of the locals' destructive nature. Crops destroyed, farms burned, and people killed. They know that no one else will protect them."

Becker turned away from the window and asked, "When will we hit the field again?"

"Just as soon as we get everyone signed up, a complete roster logged into the computer, and make sure that everyone has a rifle."

"Where we going?" asked Becker.

Now O'Neill moved around and sat behind the desk. There was a hard-copy map sitting on the desktop. It showed the major areas of human population and the few concentrations of the locals.

"Seems that there is a migration of sorts underway." O'Neill pointed to the map. "Looks like a big bunch of them are holing up along the river. We could find two, three hundred of them all at once."

"Can we handle that many of them?" asked Becker.

O'Neill gestured at the window. "By noon we'll have six hundred signed. That'll be more than enough to handle anything they throw at us. Hell, six hundred of our militia could destroy ten times that many of the enemy in a fight. They don't understand how to do it."

Becker walked across the floor and opened the door so that he could see down the stairs. The people were lined up in the hallway, waiting to enter and give their names to the recruiters there.

"You should be more than a captain," he said without turning. "Three companies at least. A battalion. You should be a lieutenant colonel."

"Of course," agreed O'Neill. "Do you want to command a company as a captain or be my executive officer as a major?"

"Major," said Becker. "I'll be a major. If I want to command a company, I can do that later."

"Good thinking." O'Neill stood up. He now wore a blue jean jacket, blue jeans and a faded blue work shirt. Pinned to the shoulders of the jacket were two yellow strips that were reminiscent of the shoulder straps worn by the calvary of the old United States Army. The silver bars of a captain were drawn in by hand. He'd have to change that.

"Let's go see how the army is shaping up. Maybe we can hit the field sooner than I thought."

Nast had not wanted to meet with Clovers or Starling. He had wanted to ignore them because he knew they were bringing bad news. They'd said that the night before. But he couldn't stop them now.

Sitting behind his desk, he pointed at the two chairs and said, "Please. Sit down."

Starling did as told but Clovers couldn't do it. He had to remain on his feet, pacing. He let Starling do the talking for both of them.

"We went out there, to the site of the great battle," she said. "Went to see if we could determine exactly what happened there."

"You weren't concerned about the locals?" asked Nast.

"We've had no trouble with them except when they believe we have encroached on their territory. That farmer and his family who were murdered, Moody, had put his farm on one of their sacred lands. Didn't do it on purpose, but did it nonetheless. That's probably why he was attacked and killed."

"You're saying he brought it on himself," said Nast.

"That doesn't matter," said Starling impatiently. "The point here is that O'Neill attacked a village and killed everyone in it. Adults, children, male and female. Killed everyone and then destroyed as much of the village as he could."

"No," said Nast, shaking his head. "I told him not to do that. I was very clear on that point."

Clovers whirled and nearly shouted. "You saying that we're lying about this?"

Nast held up his hands as if to ward off a physical blow. "No. No. I'm merely saying that I told him that I didn't want a wholesale slaughter. A punitive strike, if we could determine the guilty party or parties, but not a general strike against any individuals they came across."

Starling leaned forward, her hands on Nast's desk. "You want to hear about what we saw? About this great, pitched battle that O'Neill was describing last night?"

"Not really," said Nast, fearing the worst.

"I wondered why he didn't have much in the way of casualties. You don't fight a pitched battle without losing a few people yourself. Unless there is something that you don't tell."

"What do you want me to do?" asked Nast tiredly. "What can I do?"

Clovers said, "You're the one who authorized the militia. They operate using your authority. Revoke their commission and order them disbanded."

"I can't do that."

"Sure you can," said Clovers. "Just grab the keyboard and do it. Easy."

"You were at the show last night," said Nast. "You saw the response of the people. We're caught in a situation where they want something done. They don't know what, but it has to be something. Right or wrong, it has to be done. O'Neill is doing something. He's not filing reports, making studies, or informing a higher authority. He's in the field doing something that can be seen. Something with immediate results."

"So what?" snapped Clovers.

Nast consciously kept his temper in check. A shouting match with his subordinates would accomplish nothing. Thinking about it for a moment, he said, "What kind of people immigrated here? Came to live here?"

"What are you talking about?" asked Starling.

"Think about it. The people who made the effort to come here, who severed their ties with their home world and launched themselves into space. What kind of people were they?"

"It makes no difference," said Clovers.

"No," said Nast. "It's the point. They were self-reliant people. People who wanted something better for themselves and their children, and who were willing to risk everything for the chance. They were gamblers and adventurers and people of action."

"Again," said Clovers now weary. "So what?"

"They are not people to sit back while we talk of colonial investigations and fact-finding expeditions. They are not people who will sit back to wait to see if we work out the problem. They'll take matters into their own hands and act on what they think is the proper solution."

"You're talking in circles," said Clovers.

"No, I'm providing you with an analysis of why we can do nothing to stop O'Neill. He has the support of the people. He's out to end a problem. A very real and, in some cases, a very deadly problem. They see the action and they want a part of it."

"They can't massacre the locals," said Clovers.

"They don't see it as a massacre. It was retribution for hostile acts. O'Neill did something positive . . ."

"Positive!" shouted Clovers. "How can you call a massacre positive?"

"I meant that he took action while all we did was issue a report and request assistance from the military. Nothing positive came from that. Paper was shuffled, computer files manipulated, and no military forces have arrived."

"So you let O'Neill organize his private army that has to be approaching a thousand individuals. And while they're out eliminating the so-called enemy, no farm work is being accomplished. No exports for the few ships that call on our port facilities," said Starling.

Nast looked at her and then up at Clovers, who was still walking in small circles, trying to burn off his nervous energy. He asked them, "What would you do?"

"Order the militia disbanded," said Clovers.

"And if they refuse to obey the order?"

"Revoke our support. No pay and no expenses. They're on their own."

Nast shook his head. "You think that's going to bother them now? It's too late for that."

"Then call for regular military support," said Starling.

"It's on its way. But they're still in space."

"We've got to do something," said Starling. "We just can't sit back while an armed force roams the land killing everything it doesn't like."

Nast had to grin. They had just walked into the trap that he had been laying for them. "Act now, you say. Make a positive move whether it's right or wrong?"

Starling slumped into her chair and Clovers stopped pacing. "I take your meaning," said Clovers.

"You want positive action?" asked Nast, "then I'll give you something to do. Last night's show was a result of O'Neill's positive action and his unchallenged statements that they met with a force of enemy soldiers. Get the evidence that it was a peaceful village. A video of it. Pictures of the children who were killed."

"No one's going to believe it," said Clovers.

"Right now that doesn't matter. Gather the evidence. O'Neill will deny it but there are others who were there. Get a few of them to confirm the video and you begin to build your case. That's how you're going to stop O'Neill."

"Maybe the colonial office would like a representative to travel with O'Neill," said Starling. "Someone to observe what is happening with him."

"That's not a bad idea," said Nast.

"I'll do it," said Clovers.

"Why?" asked Starling. "It was my idea, and he's got women in his militia. I'll do it."

"Starling, you join the militia," said Nast. "Clovers. Get a video team and return to the village. Get everything on tape. Take a doctor to talk about the injuries. Get everything you can. Once we have the evidence gathered, we'll make a planetwide broadcast of it." He looked up at them waiting for one of them to speak.

"Positive action," said Clovers. "It's not much but at least it's something."

The lines still stretched out the building and down the block, but Starling didn't want to stand in them. It was too hot and humid outside. Besides, she was an official of the colonial government and didn't have to wait with the peasants. She pushed her way to the front of the line and grabbed the door.

A beefy hand shot out and a voice demanded, "Where do you think you're going, sister?"

"I'm Leigh Starling. Colonial office and I have official business here."

"Fucking colonial office," said another. "Not worth the effort to blow it up."

Starling opened the door and found that it wasn't that much cooler inside. Had to be a result of the constant traffic in and out of the building. The air-conditioning couldn't handle the load.

There was a man sitting behind a desk to one side. He seemed to be taking notes on everything that was happening in the hall. He looked up as she approached. "Yeah?"

"I want to see O'Neill."

He stared at her with distaste. "Join the line."

"I have official business with O'Neill."

"Does Colonel O'Neill know about this official business?" the man asked.

"No." She hesitated. "Colonel? Last night he was a captain."

"Last night we had a single company. This morning we have a regiment. A colonel commands a regiment."

Starling couldn't help herself. She grinned at that. "Well, I'd like to see Colonel O'Neill on official colonial business as soon as possible."

The man glanced at the papers in front of him and then called, "Corporal Boyle. Take this woman to the colonel but see that she doesn't bother him. When she's finished, bring her back and escort her out."

"Yes, sir." He looked at Starling. "Follow me."

They climbed the stairs, reached a second-floor office, and stopped outside the door. The corporal knocked and then waited. A moment later the door opened. Starling recognized the man as Becker. He was in a makeshift uniform with major's leaves drawn on the yellow straps on the shoulders of his denim jacket.

"What?"

"Sir, the lady has requested a meeting with the colonel."

Becker said, "About what?"

"I'll discuss it with O'Neill."

"Colonel O'Neill is very busy at the moment. As his executive officer, it is my function to relieve him of the annoying duties of dealing with civilians."

"I'm from the colonial office and I have business with the colonel." She felt silly saying those words. In fact, she hadn't thought much about what she as going to do. She'd planned on showing up and joining up but now worried that she wouldn't be able to get away with that. She doubted they were turning away anyone, but they might not want a woman from the colonial office. Now it was too late to do anything about it.

Becker studied her, grinned, and said, "I'll see if the colonel has a couple of minutes for you." He closed the door quietly.

Starling folded her arms and leaned against the wall. She studied the corporal. A young man with shaggy hair. He wore the standard issue coveralls, but had two black stripes drawn on the sleeves to show his rank. She thought about making conversation but the corporal, who might have been nineteen or twenty, didn't seem to want to talk.

The door opened again and Becker gestured to her. To Boyle, he said, "You can return to your duties."

"I was told to wait for her."

"Your orders have been changed by the colonel. You have a problem with that?"

"No, sir. Thank you, sir."

Starling entered the room and looked at O'Neill. He seemed to have grown since the night before. He seemed to be larger than he had been. Strength seemed to surround him like an aura. Suddenly she understood what Nast had been trying to say. This was a natural leader who would inspire loyalty in those around him. It was more than just taking action. It was something about the man too, as if he was bigger than life.

"We have a great deal to do here," he said looking at her.

Starling lifted a hand and wiped her lips, surprised to find sweat beaded there. She hesitated, unsure of what to say.

"Come on, woman," said Becker. "We don't have all day. We've a great deal of work before we hit the field."

Starling kept her eyes on O'Neill. He returned her gaze and finally smiled. "We've a moment, Major." He gestured at one of the chairs opposite him. "Please. Sit down."

Starling did and finally found her tongue. "I've come to join."

"Oh, good Christ," said Becker. "You could have done that downstairs. You don't have to bother us with that."

"I'm with the colonial office," she said.

O'Neill nodded. "What's their reaction to what we're doing here?"

She found herself speaking without thinking about it. "They're, Nast, is worried about the outcome. He doesn't want to see a massacre anywhere."

"He told me the same thing, but if you're going into the field for retribution, then someone is going to die."

"Maybe you're a little hard on that retribution thing," said Starling.

"This is not a conflict that we started, but once we're involved, we have to see it through. We have no choice in the matter."

She started to say that there was no conflict but realized that she would be arguing against her own inclusion in the army. If she didn't believe in the cause, why was she there?

And then easily, it came to her. Turn the argument around on them. Use the words that had been spoken by Nast and Clovers. That was the ticket.

To O'Neill, she said, "The colonial office shuffles paper and makes studies but doesn't do anything that is positive. We talk and plan and then do nothing. Here is an opportunity to do something."

O'Neill nodded at that and then grinned broadly. "Have you any special training?"

Starling shrugged. "Just what I learned in college and the various diplomatic schools I attended. Learned how to survey land, to evaluate its potential for colonization and the like. Everything was geared to a career in the colonial office."

"Well," said O'Neill, "such talents can be channeled into paths that are more beneficial for us. Many civilian skills, when applied properly, can be used for a military occupation."

"I suppose . . ."

O'Neill stood and walked around to sit on the front of the desk. "An engineer, for example. He can build bridges in the civilian world. He knows their strengths and their weaknesses. He knows many things about them that could be applied to destroying them if necessary. He would know that dropping the span into the river is not as damaging as destroying the abutments that hold the spans. He would know where to place the explosives to do the most damage."

"Sure," said Starling. "But I'm not an engineer."

"No, but your talents could be put to use in Intelligence. What is military intelligence anyway? It is the skills to learn about the enemy and apply that knowledge to hurt him. Your skills would make you a good intelligence officer."

"I don't know about that," she said.

"I do," said O'Neill. "If you're interested, you may join the command as a captain in charge of intelligence."

Starling couldn't believe her luck. It was the best position for her to be in. She nodded slowly and said, "I would be happy to join as the intelligence officer."

"Good," said O'Neill clapping his hands. "It's settled. There is a wide variety of intelligence that we could use. Anything that pertains to the locals, societal habits, abilities, and most importantly, locations of their villages in the area."

"I don't know . . ."

"Are you with us or against us?" asked O'Neill.

"With you, of course," she said quickly. "But I don't want to see a slaughter of the locals."

"And I don't want to see a slaughter of humans," said O'Neill. "That's all we're trying to accomplish here. The protection of the human inhabitants of Delta Royal Three. That's our whole mission."

"Yes, sir," said Starling standing.

"Fine. Major Becker will get you the proper insignia and provide a uniform jacket. I'll expect a complete briefing on the enemy's capabilities this evening."

"I'll need to use the colonial office files to gain access to the information."

"I don't have a problem with that. Just don't tell them much about our operation."

"Yes, sir." She didn't know whether to salute or not. Then, figuring it wouldn't hurt, she lifted her hand to her forehead.

"Major Becker will teach you how to salute later. Until then, please don't try again."

Starling hesitated and O'Neill said nothing more, so she left the office. She couldn't believe her luck. She'd be on the staff where she could watch everything closely. As she walked down the stairs, she suddenly wondered if she'd been tricked. She'd be on the staff where O'Neill could watch her. It made for an interesting guessing game.

13

FLAGSHIP OF THE TENTH INTERPLANETARY INFANTRY REGIMENT

THE TWO COMPANIES that were to be deployed, along with the attached platoon, stood in the shuttle bay waiting for orders to board the craft. It was not a formal deployment, with flags and bands and a reviewing stand. It was Jefferson and Torrence standing at the head of the formation while the rest of the provisional battalion stood at attention waiting for their orders to be issued.

"Sorry to have bumped this up," said Jefferson, "but I don't like the way things look on the planet's surface."

"First thing we'll do is rein in that militia," said Torrence. "Never saw a makeshift militia that didn't collapse when the real military arrived. They'll all want to get back to their farms and families. This is the excuse."

"I know the theory," said Jefferson. "I'm just not sure how this—what is he now, a general?—O'Neill will react. Looks like he'll be able to hold his militia together with a force of will."

"With us around, there will be no reason for their militia."

Jefferson nodded and looked beyond her, at the special platoon. "You had much to do with them?"

"Not since you changed the orders. I wish we could keep them here for another week or so of indoctrination."

"If they give you trouble, report it to me and I'll recall them."

"Yes, sir."

Torrence looked into his eyes then. She lowered her voice so that the staff who was there wouldn't be able to hear. The conversation was turning private.

"It was good last night," she said.

"Very good." Jefferson let his mind wander. After he'd issued the new orders and saw that everyone was working to carry them out, he and Torrence had decided that a private conference was needed. They had walked away from the provisional battalion, down the corridors, and to the elevator. Jefferson's plan was to hold the meeting in his cabin, away from the prying eyes of all the others.

John, Six One Two, had followed him without him knowing it. They, Jefferson and Torrence, had stopped in the corridor outside his cabin. There were no guards on duty. No one in the corridor as Jefferson had turned and found Torrence grabbing at him, pulling him close. She kissed him, her tongue pressing at his mouth and then at his tongue. She had broken the kiss and grinned up at him.

"Let's get inside," he'd said.

"Of course."

As he touched the button at the side of the hatch, he'd heard a sound and turned. John, Six One Two, was standing there, near the elevator.

"You think he saw anything?" asked Torrence.

Keeping his voice low, Jefferson had said. "That's what you get for a public display of affection."

"I thought the corridor was empty."

"So did I." Jefferson glanced back and raised his voice. "Something I can do for you, Lieutenant?"

"Yes, sir." He started walking forward, picking up the pace as he got closer. He stopped and saluted. "Colonel, Lieutenant Smith, John, Six One Two, requests permission to speak."

"Permission granted."

John, Six One Two, relaxed slightly. "Thank you, sir. I wanted to ask for permission for my platoon to deploy later."

Jefferson raised his eyebrows. "Why's that?"

"Sir, I don't believe that we've had the proper indoctrination."

Jefferson turned on Torrence. "You put him up to this, Major?"

"No, sir."

"Sir. I have been assigned to this platoon for a long time and I know what the level of training is. All our training to this point has been theory. No fact. No interaction with units other than my own. I think we need a chance to learn how to work with a larger unit."

"Lieutenant," said Jefferson, "I don't believe that we have a choice in this matter and I'm not convinced that another week, or two weeks, is going to be of benefit. You learn best by doing. You will deploy."

"Yes, sir. Sorry to bother you, sir." He stepped back and saluted. "Thank you, sir."

John, Six One Two, had disappeared a moment later. Torrence watched the elevator doors close behind him and then said, "I think he caught us."

"You might be right, but it doesn't matter."

Now, standing on the deck of the shuttle bay, with the provisional battalion, its attached platoon, and everything else, Jefferson was wondering if it did matter. If the lieutenant would be spreading the gossip to his fellows.

Torrence leaned close to him and said, "Guess I better join the battalion."

"We'll be watching closely from here."

"And I appreciate that." She turned formally and said, as she saluted, "Is that all, sir?"

"Certainly." Jefferson returned the salute. "Good luck. Join your battalion Major."

"Yes, sir." Torrence did an about face and walked swiftly across the shuttle-bay deck. She centered herself on the battalion, let Martuesi salute, returned it, and said, "Join your company."

"Yes, ma'am."

Jefferson watched Torrence, her back to him, as she surveyed the provisional battalion. Most of them were battle-tested troops. Good troops. Martuesi was new, but she had been well-trained. The only question was the new platoon, and it shouldn't cause that much trouble.

Torrence issued her orders, her voice carrying and echoing in the shuttle bay. The company commanders saluted and turned, passing on the instructions. The formation began to break up as the men and women boarded the shuttles. These looked like thick airliners, designed to operate inside a planet's atmosphere.

Music boomed out suddenly as the controllers in the booth played the tape. The soldiers picked up the rhythm of the music as they marched to the shuttles.

Torrence turned, looked at Jefferson, and threw him another salute. Jefferson returned it and waited as the battalion disappeared into the shuttles.

After several minutes, most of the battalion had boarded the shuttles. One of the staff officers said, "We're going to have to clear the shuttle bay."

"Right," said Jefferson. Still he didn't move. He felt guilty about letting them go. He always felt that he was ordering his soldiers to their deaths while he stayed behind on the ship, comfortable and air-conditioned. He knew it wasn't true, and that as the commander, his duty was often to remain behind, but that didn't mean he had to like it.

Torrence was the last one to enter the shuttle. As she did, the maintenance crew swarmed out, closed up the hatches and doors, and then pulled the last of the covers from the inlets, engine exhausts and instrument ports.

"Please clear the shuttle bay," boomed a voice from the control room.

Jefferson turned and walked to the hatch. He stopped, let one of the other officers open it, and then exited. As soon as they closed the hatch, the light above it turned red, telling everyone that the air was being evacuated from the shuttle bay.

"We can watch the launch from the observation bay," said an officer.

"No," said Jefferson. "I'll be on the bridge with Captain Clemens. Make sure that Carter is in the intell shop and have him report to me."

"Yes, sir."

"Have the commo officer contact that Commissioner Nast on the planet's surface and let him know that our people are on the way."

"Yes, sir."

Jefferson was silent for a moment and then said, "Have

Carter locate that militia regiment. I want them under surveillance as much as possible."

"Problem there is that we don't have satellites in the planet's atmosphere."

"I didn't ask for excuses," said Jefferson. "Deploy probes if necessary."

"Yes, sir."

Jefferson glanced at the others and then began to walk along the corridor heading for the bridge.

O'Neill held up a hand to stop the column of ATVs. Now there were more than two hundred of them rolling over the open ground, creating a cloud of dust that reached a thousand feet into the bright morning sky. He stood up, and then leaped over the side of the vehicle, hitting the ground. He turned and moved back along the column, searching for his staff officers.

In the second ATV was Becker. The major sat in the front seat. The windshield had been lowered but Becker wore goggles. As O'Neill approached, he grabbed the goggles and slipped them down around his neck so that he looked like a tank commander from the German Afrika Corps during War Two.

"Officer's call in ten minutes," said O'Neill. "At the lead vehicle."

"Yes, sir."

O'Neill turned and walked back. He pulled the map out of the case that he'd tossed into the rear, and opened it. In the war videos, the commander spread the map out on the hood of his jeep or truck or tank, but the ATV didn't have much of a hood. Just a sloped area in front that kept the mud from splashing up to cover the windshield.

"Help me with this," he said to the driver.

"Yes, sir."

Becker and Starling arrived. O'Neill looked at her. "Show me that concentration of the beasts."

Starling moved around and touched the map. It showed a partial desert, not a sand-and-cactus desert, but one of little rain, tough grass, and stunted trees. At the edge of it was a wide river that looked almost like a line drawn on a map to show borders between two countries.

"The latest intelligence puts them there, but they're mobile and might have moved on by now."

"But they haven't," said O'Neill.

"No, sir, there have been no indications that they will have moved on."

Other officers joined them. Jones, Byrd, Primmer, and Davis. The first sergeant, Pruggs, also came forward. They clustered around, facing the map.

"I make it another day to the location," said O'Neill. "But I think we should throw out some scouts. Anyone familiar with this section of the planet should be drafted for that." He looked at Starling. "Tell them."

Starling wiped the sweat from her face. Her hand was gritty from the dust kicked up by the ATVs' tires. "We believe that this is a yearly meeting. Biggest of the meetings the locals . . ."

"Enemy," snapped O'Neill.

"Enemy," corrected Starling, "hold. Our information puts them on the river in this general location but they could move along the river in either direction."

"Hence the scouts," said O'Neill. "We catch them here and we can break their back."

"There'll be other congregations," said Becker.

"Maybe. But we do enough damage to this one and they'll think twice before they get together again."

"You sure this is a good idea?" asked Starling. "This could escalate into a real war."

"They started it," said O'Neill. "Don't forget that."

"Yes, sir."

"I want to make another hundred miles before we camp tonight," said O'Neill. "No fires tonight. I want nothing that could be spotted. We'll just have to rough it this once."

"Yes, sir."

O'Neill rubbed a hand through his sweat-soaked hair. "I know some of the boys have radios to keep in touch with home. Up till now it didn't matter, but I don't want them transmitting anymore. That can be traced."

"Yes, sir," said Becker.

"The locals can't do that," said Starling.

"Good operational security is not based on what you think the enemy can do. Why take unnecessary chances with it?" asked O'Neill. "Anything else?"

O'Neill checked the time. "That's given the soldiers about a fifteen-minute rest stop. Let's get going again."

"Yes, sir."

As soon as the shuttles had touched down and rolled to a stop, Torrence was off. There was a delegation from the colonial office to meet them, but she ignored the officials until she saw that the battalion officers were getting the equipment, the floaters, and the other gear out of the shuttle. Satisfied with that, she walked over to the delegation.

"I'm Major Victoria Torrence, Tenth Interplanetary Infantry," she said.

"Nast. Colonial Office. We're glad that you're here."

"I've got a pretty good idea about the problem," said Torrence. "Our major concern is that regiment formed by one Richard O'Neill."

"Under my orders," said Nast.

Torrence surveyed the man slowly. Typical planetary bureaucrat. Self-important but without the intelligence to think for himself.

"Your orders include the hunting of the local population? There is a treaty in effect here."

Nast seemed to grow red in the face. Sweat beaded on his forehead and dripped. It looked as if they could fry eggs on his skin.

"Don't you tell me my job," he said. "I know my function and I know yours. You're here to take my orders, not make accusations."

"No," said Torrence, shaking her head. "I'm here to restore order and make sure that everyone, you, me, the farmers, the immigrants, and the natives, especially the natives, get a fair shake. That's my job."

"We'll see about that," said Nast. "I'll be putting in a call to your commander just as soon as I can."

"Fine. In the meantime, do you have quarters arranged for my battalion?"

"Nothing was said about quarters. I thought soldiers stayed in tents or sleep on the ground."

"When there's a reason to. What kind of facilities can you offer?"

"There are the dormitories used by immigrants when they first arrive. Nothing fancy."

"That'll be fine. My officers and I will want a briefing on the situation as soon as you can arrange it."

"I'd have thought you'd want to get into the field as quickly as possible," said Nast.

"And do what?" asked Torrence.

"Whatever it is that soldiers do."

She smiled patiently. "Well, we like to understand the situation before we run off to do something. Once we understand it, we can plan an effective course of action. One that will minimize the casualties to us and reduce the damage that we do here."

Nast glanced to the rear, where a number of his people stood. He'd planted Starling on O'Neill's staff. It only made good sense to plant someone on Torrence's staff. He could monitor everyone, file his reports to the colonial office and have enough information to shortstop any questions directed at him. He would be able to blame Torrence, or O'Neill, or the locals. He would come out smelling like a rose.

"I believe that Mister Clovers can assist you. If that will be satisfactory?"

"Fine. I want a complete set of the local maps and charts. Those with the latest data on them."

"I would think that your ship could provide you with that information."

"It could," said Torrence, "but the mapping survey could take two or three weeks. If you have the information already, then we could save some time."

"I'll have Clovers deliver the information. Now, if there is nothing else, I have work to do."

"Fine," said Torrence. She turned her back on the man, dismissing him. She knew that she was walking a fine line, but she couldn't let a bureaucrat think that he had the upper hand. If he believed it, he could make life miserable.

The unloading of the shuttles was going well. The troops were out and the equipment was being marshalled according to a plan that had been created by the ship's computers.

Torrence wanted to do something more, to take charge, but knew enough to leave them alone. Sometimes an officer could do too much commanding. If the operation was running smoothly, why get in there to create havoc?

To herself, she said, "Well, you're down now. Let's see if you can keep from screwing it up too badly."

14

DELTA ROYAL THREE

JOHN, SIX ONE TWO, stood at the end of the squad bay and watched as his platoon worked to clean their equipment. That was the thing he'd learned in the hypno tanks. When there was nothing else to do, when they had to stay close but there was no chance of danger, have the troops clean the weapons. No one ever got killed because his or her weapon was too clean.

Sara, Six One Three walked the length of the bay slowly, glancing right and left to make sure that everyone was working hard. There were a few mumbled complaints, but nothing that required a response.

As she reached the far end, she grinned at John, Six One Two, and said, "We are now in the field."

"I wish there had been more time."

"Four years of training is a long time to prepare. It's good to have the opportunity to use the training."

John, Six One Two, shrugged. "I suppose so. I just wish I felt better about it."

"We could prepare forever and still think we're not ready," said Sara, Six One Three.

"Yes." John, Six One Two, studied her for a moment. It was almost like looking into a mirror. "Leave the first squad leader in charge and then join me."

"Yes, sir," she said. She walked into the squad bay and gave

111

the squad leaders their instructions. When she returned, she asked, "Where are we going?"

"Away for a few minutes," said John, Six One Two. "We rarely get the opportunity to get away."

"Certainly. But I should let the squad leaders know just in case something happens."

John, Six One Two, touched the small radio receiver attached to his belt. "We'll know before they do and besides, we're not going that far."

"Yes, sir."

John, Six One Two, turned and left the second floor. He descended the stairs, turned to the right and opened a door. He waved Sara, Six One Three, inside. It was an individual room with a cot, chair, lamp, and a view screen that could pick up the planetary broadcasts, or be used as the VTD for a computer if the keyboard was plugged in.

"My quarters," he said.

Sara, Six One Three, nodded, entered, and walked to the chair, sitting down. She leaned back in it and closed her eyes, visibly relaxing. "It's good to get away from the platoon once in a while."

John, Six One Two, followed her in, closed the door and then sat on the cot. He rubbed a hand over his face. He didn't say anything to her. He just looked at her, staring, as if he'd never seen her before. Suddenly he was conscious of the differences in their bodies. The curves, the swellings, the lack of facial hair. Little things that underscored the differences between boys and girls.

Sara, Six One Three, opened her eyes and said, "I never realized how much pressure there was. Constantly under the scrutiny of the others. They're waiting for me to make a mistake. Any mistake, no matter how small."

"How do you know?"

She grinned. "Because I'm waiting for you to make a mistake. I think I resent your command because the only difference is that you're a minute older than me. Just one minute."

"There are other differences," said John, Six One Two.

"Nothing of consequence."

"You're a girl and I'm a boy."

"Sure," she said, shrugging. "But that doesn't make you superior. The only real difference is that you're older."

"And stronger."

"Not necessarily," said Sara, Six One Three.

"I could prove it to you."

"How?"

John, Six One Two, stood and pushed the cot to one side, up against the wall. He held out a hand and said, "Stand up."

Sara, Six One Three, complied. Then she pushed the chair toward the cot. She lifted it up and set it on the mattress. "What do you have in mind?"

"Wrestling. I'll prove that I'm stronger than you."

"Okay," she said, grinning. "But we've done this a dozen times. Strength doesn't mean that much. It's endurance and leverage and understanding the opponent."

"And strength," said John, Six One Two. He got down on his hands and knees. "I'll give you the top first."

Sara, Six One Three, got down, leaned across his back, putting one hand around his waist, and then reached forward to grip his right arm near the elbow. "Whenever you're ready," she said.

For a moment, John, Six One Two, didn't move. He took in the sensations. Her hips pressed against him. Her breasts on his back. He was aware that she was a girl. Fully aware of it as he had never been before. The image of Jefferson and Torrence in the corridor near the colonel's cabin flashed. Them facing each other, kissing.

"You ready?" asked Sara, Six One Three.

"Sure." He let his elbow collapse, rolled to the left, away from her and reached up, grabbing at her shoulders. He pulled her down on top of him so that they were face to face. She tried to break his hold but he wrapped his legs around her hips, holding her tightly. He wasn't interested in the pin or fighting back, only holding onto her.

Sara, Six One Three's face was only inches from his. He could feel her breath on his neck. He could look into her eyes and watched as something changed there suddenly. The twisting stopped and she seemed to freeze.

"What?" she asked.

"I . . ." John, Six One Two, didn't know what he wanted to say. He had always believed that the commander had to remain aloof. He couldn't engage in the horseplay with the troops because the commander didn't do things like that. He could display no emotion and no affection. That was what the tapes had told him since the moment he had entered training. But Jefferson and Torrence had shattered that belief with their actions in the corridor before planetfall.

John, Six One Two, was aware of everything about her body. He relaxed slightly, letting his legs fall back to the floor. She shifted around so that one of his legs was caught between hers.

"This isn't right," said Sara, Six One Three, but she made no move to get up.

"Why?"

"I don't know. It just seems to be wrong. We shouldn't be here, together like this, while the others are working."

That wasn't what John, Six One Two, had wanted to hear. But then he didn't know what he wanted to hear. Almost from the moment of his birth, he had been separated from the others. He had been alone at the top of the command pyramid. He'd watched the others playing together, working together, and wished that he could join them. But he never had. He'd stayed on the sidelines as all the instructors, teachers, tapes, and manuals had demanded of him.

They were frozen in time. Neither of them moving. John, Six One Two, felt his emotions slip and slide as he tried to figure out what he felt and what he said. He was acutely aware that the woman was his sister, more than his sister, but he wasn't sure that mattered. Not given the fact that they were almost identical except for the differences created by their sexes.

This was a moment that he didn't want to end. He wanted to clutch his sister, hold her tightly and take strength from her. There was so many things that he didn't understand, that he had not been taught. From the moment that he was born, his training had gone in one direction. There was no time wasted on the social skills that would be of no use to the combat commander.

Sara, Six One Three, who had been slightly tense, suddenly relaxed completely. John, Six One Two, felt the tension drain from her. She laid her head on his shoulder and seemed to hold him tighter.

"We shouldn't," she said.

John, Six One Two, didn't know what she meant. The vision of the naked lieutenant in his cabin sprang to mind. He remembered his sudden response to seeing her standing there nude. And he remembered her in the observation deck. His body had responded to her presence in ways that he didn't understand. In that respect his education was sorely lacking.

Sara, Six One Three, shifted around again, still lying on top of him. She moved her legs so that both of his were between hers. He felt his body react. His breathing came in short gasps as if he had run a long distance. He was lightheaded and perspiring.

"This is not right," she said again.

But John, Six One Two, didn't understand that. He could see nothing wrong in what they were doing. Holding each other. The physical presence of her was enough for him for the moment. He wanted to stay with her. Form a closer relationship to her as some of the enlisted men and women had done. It was only responsibility that kept them apart.

"The platoon," she said.

John, Six One Two, nodded and knew that they would have to leave. They had to get back to work. He let go of her, but she didn't move. She held onto him for another minute before she looked at him.

"We've been lied to," she said.

"How?"

"All the tapes that said we could never show emotion or affection were wrong. If we don't, then we're no better than savages." She looked into his eyes. "I've always felt sorry for you?"

"Why?"

"You were the oldest, separated by an accident of selection. Born five minutes later and you would have been allowed to mix in the fun."

"I didn't think anyone noticed."

"We all noticed," she said. "Shelia, Seven Four Eight, and Timothy, Seven One One, and I have talked about it. We wanted to invite you to join us but never did. Didn't think it would be right."

"You should have," said John, Six One Two, quietly. "It might not have been right, but you should have."

Suddenly she grinned. "You see? This planetfall hasn't been all bad. We've learned something already. We haven't gotten into the field but we've learned something."

"If only we'd done it before," said John, Six One Two.

"There's time now." She sat up, moved around, and put a hand on his shoulder. "Join us tonight, in the squad bay, or rather, in the NCO quarters."

"I'm supposed to remain here," said John, Six One Two.

Sara, Six One Three, shook her head. "Major Torrence is not going to be separated from her company and Captain Martuesi will be with her company. No reason for you not to join us."

He was quiet, thinking, and finally he nodded. "I'll move my gear."

Sara, Six One Three, leaped to her feet and said, "I'll help." Then she looked at him strangely. "What was that about wrestling."

"I don't know," said John, Six One Two. "It was just . . . the only time I was allowed to touch anyone was during the hand-to-hand training. Wrestling was the best of it."

Her voice lowered and she said, "I just never understood. I should have but didn't."

"It's okay now," said John, Six One Two. "We both understand it now."

Garvey had haunted the personnel office, demanding to see files that the S-1, Captain Winston, had told him were privileged documents. While they weren't exactly classified, they weren't available for general distribution either.

"I just want to see them," said Garvey. "Check a few facts out against what I've been told."

"You willing to compromise?" asked Winston.

"Always."

"Off the record, you could ask me the questions and then I could verify the information for you."

Garvey shook his head. "It would be better if I could do it myself. I won't quote the source and I won't look into any one of the files too deeply. Besides, Colonel Jefferson wants you to cooperate with me."

"You have permission from the colonel?" asked Winston.

"Well, honestly, no. But I could ask him and I'm sure that he would suggest you cooperate."

Winston had to laugh. "I'm sure the colonel would tell me to cooperate as long as I was not violating any regulations. He wouldn't tell me to hand everything to you on a platter."

"I suppose you're right, but then what harm could I do?"

"There is no telling what harm you could do," said Winston. "The power of the press is sometimes amazing."

"Then you won't let me see the records."

"Tell me what you want," said Winston.

Garvey clapped his hands together and rubbed them like a man about to dig into a Thanksgiving feast. "I would like to see the files on that new platoon."

"Can't help you with that," said Winston.

"I thought we had worked that out."

"Not with them. They're a breed apart. Their records are not filed here because they're a special unit. I have only the records of the permanent party assigned to the Tenth Interplanetary Infantry Regiment."

"Then who would have them?"

Winston shrugged. "Major Torrence may have them in her files. They may be stored with the ship's personnel officer, or Colonel Jefferson might control them himself."

"Great."

"Colonel Jefferson is in the communications center now, I believe," said Winston.

"Thanks." Garvey knew a dismissal when he heard one. He left the personnel section, entered the corridor. He walked down it slowly, noticing that things had changed subtly now that there were soldiers on a planet's surface. Some of the games played during the long voyages through space were gone. The guards that sometimes lined the corridors had been relieved. The ship's lights, which during the day glowed bright white, had been dimmed slightly as if to save power. Unused and unimportant sections of the ship had been shut down so that all power could be diverted into the weapons systems in case they were needed.

He reached the elevator and took it up toward the command level. He walked past the intelligence, plans, training sections, and administrative sections commanded by the exec when she was on the ship. Communications was near the bridge. Garvey stopped in front of the hatch, but it didn't automatically open as it usually did. Instead a voice said, "State your business please."

"Is Colonel Jefferson there?"

An instant later came the response. "Jefferson here."

"Colonel, I've a matter to discuss with you."

"And I suppose it is so important that it can't wait until a little later."

"Up to you, Colonel."

"Wait one."

There was a metallic click and then the hatch opened. Garvey started to step through, but Jefferson stopped him, pushing him back. Jefferson entered the corridor and the hatch was closed behind him.

"You know," said Garvey, "that makes me very suspicious. What are you hearing on the radio that you don't want me to hear?"

"So far," said Jefferson, "there hasn't been a damned thing. All routine." Then he grinned. "Except that Major Torrence has managed to piss off the local colonial representative already. Within minutes of landing actually. I'm rather proud of her for that."

"Colonial rep was the one that asked for your help," Garvey reminded him.

"Which isn't to say the man did us a favor. Now, what is it that you wanted that is critical?"

"I'm interested in doing a feature on that new platoon of yours. Several interesting angles to be explored, from the fact they're all obviously brothers and sisters to the fact they have all been assigned to the same unit."

"I'm not convinced that the headquarters would be thrilled with a report on them. At least not yet. And, so far, they haven't done a thing."

"Still," said Garvey, "you have to admit they're interesting. I talked to your personnel officer, Winston, and he told me their records were filed away. Not with the rest of the regiment's. Is that unusual?"

Jefferson shrugged. "I've never had a special unit attached before. Their records are all together and Major Torrence was doing something with them."

"Mind if I take a look at them?"

Jefferson rubbed his chin with a finger, thinking. "I can't think of a reason that you'd need to see them."

"Any reason for me not to see them?"

"Well, personal files are not public property," said Jefferson. "Not like many of the documents that we generate. Freedom of information clashes with privacy."

"There's something mighty strange about that platoon," said Garvey. He stood waiting.

Jefferson finally nodded. "Okay. You and I will go take a quick look at them. I say stop and we stop."

"Let's go," said Garvey.

Together they walked to the administration section. The NCOIC was still there. He hadn't deployed with Torrence. Since it was a combat mission and not an administrative one, he remained behind to take care of the regiment's routine business.

When Jefferson entered the office, the man climbed to his feet and said, "Good afternoon, Colonel. How may I be of assistance?"

The office was a dark room with a bank of computer screens built into a series of desks. Two clerks worked at two of the desks, adding information to the computer banks, updating files, promotion lists, and searching for the names of those eligible for various awards and decorations.

Jefferson surveyed that activity and then turned his attention on the NCO in front of him. "Sergeant?"

"Dalton, sir. James W. Dalton. NCO in charge of the admin section."

"I'd like to see the records of that new platoon. Major Torrence had them."

"Yes, sir." He looked pointedly at Garvey.

"Mister Garvey is with me."

"Yes, sir." Dalton turned and touched a computer keyboard. "You familiar with the coding system?"

Jefferson shook his head once. "You stay right here. Give us the platoon leader's file first, followed by the platoon sergeant's."

"Yes, sir." He typed for a moment and then said, "It's on the screen."

Jefferson pulled a chair around and sat down. Garvey stood behind him. Jefferson read the first page and then scrolled down, scanning. To Garvey, he said, "You want me to slow down or stop, you say so."

"Of course."

They read John, Six One Two's, file, then Sara, Six One Three's, working to the squad leaders and then the fire team leaders. They were thin files, giving some vital statistics, the military training they had received, and aptitudes that were adaptable to military specialties.

"You see anything strange here?" asked Garvey.

"No."

"They only go back seven years. Nothing about their childhood, schooling outside the military, and nothing about their birthdate."

"In a situation like this," said Jefferson, "the records we're given are often sanitized so that we don't have information that we have no need to know."

"Their schooling and birthdates?" said Garvey. "Hell, Colonel, you should be as interested in this as I am. They're assigned to your regiment."

Jefferson took his hands away from the keyboard and looked back at Garvey. "I would think that information that related to their pre-military service might have been considered irrelevant by the personnel officer who created these files. There is the data we need to evaluate their military abilities. That is what we are supposed to grade. Not their background or their schooling. Just their military abilities."

"I don't like it," said Garvey. "I don't like it one little bit."

"That's the interesting thing, Mister Garvey. You don't have to like it." Jefferson touched a button and the screen went blank.

"Hey, I'm not through."

"Yes, you are," said Jefferson. "There is nothing there. I shouldn't have shown you that much. These are not public records. Look for your story elsewhere. Now I've got work to do."

"Certainly," said Garvey. He stared at the blank screen for a minute and realized that his curiosity had not been satisfied. If anything, it had been tweaked again. He wanted to know more about the platoon and he was determined to find it.

15

DELTA ROYAL THREE

THE MAIN BODY of the assault force was hidden in the trees at the base of a large hill. The ridge line ran from north to south with little tall vegetation on it. There were thick grasses, a few bushes, and a single tree. O'Neill stood in front of what he now called the command car and looked up the hill.

The scout who stood with him glanced at the map and then back up the hill. "Party of maybe fifty of them on the other side. Camped for the night."

"Fifty?" asked O'Neill. He shot a glance at Starling and then Becker.

"Fifty total. I'd say maybe half of them are adult males. No sign of weapons other than a couple of big clubs. Might be more ceremonial than an actual weapon."

"Captain Starling," said O'Neill.

"Sir?"

"Would the enemy be carrying ceremonial clubs?"

"We have nothing in the files that suggest they have much in the way of ceremonial artifacts, but our information on them is very sketchy."

"Then your analysis is that the clubs are actual weapons and not symbolic."

"There isn't the data necessary to make a good guess either way," she said.

121

O'Neill blinked in the bright afternoon sun. Sweat beaded on his face and dripped, creating streaks in the dust. There were clean patches around his eyes where his goggles had been. He wiped his face on his sleeve.

"We have to assume that the enemy on the other side of the ridge line is hostile," said O'Neill.

The scout nodded. "Looks like they might have some equipment, some clothing, taken from some of our farms. I didn't want to get close enough to see any better. I was afraid they'd see me."

"How are they traveling?" asked O'Neill.

"On foot. Got a couple of things on poles that they drag along the ground. No wheels on it."

O'Neill turned away and rubbed the side of his face with the back of his hand. "We can't leave a force that large on our lines of communication. We're going to have to take them out."

"You can't do that," Starling said. "You can't just kill them because they're in the way."

"More than that," said O'Neill. "You heard the scout say that they had human gear and that they had weapons. This is the kind of thing we can't allow."

"You have no right. It's their planet."

"Not anymore," said O'Neill. "It's ours now. You'd better get that straight right now. And the sooner they learn it, the better off we're all going to be."

"I didn't sign on to participate in wholesale slaughter," she said.

"You are free to go," snapped O'Neill. "If you can't see the bigger picture. Get the hell out. Your services are not indispensable."

Starling stood flat-footed for a moment and then spun, stomping off, toward the ATV she used. O'Neill shook his head as she left.

"You can't let her go," said Becker quietly. "She knows too much."

I'm aware of that," said O'Neill. He turned and pointed at a burly man in dirty overalls. He wore an old cap with the three stripes of a buck sergeant drawn on it. The man ambled over.

"Henriks," said O'Neill.

"Yes, sir." The man spoke slowly, as if unsure of the words.

He needed a shave and a bath. He carried a sawed-off shotgun.

"Got a job for you. One that you'll need to take care of yourself and one that you can't tell anyone that you did."

"Yes, sir."

O'Neill looked at the scout and said, "Excuse us for a few minutes."

"Yes, sir." The scout walked away.

To Becker, O'Neill said, "You can leave too if you want to. Or stay. Up to you."

"I'll stay."

"Henriks," said O'Neill. "You know that woman that just left here."

"Yes, sir."

"Kill her."

"Yes, sir."

"Wait for her to get out of sight of the rest of the regiment and then kill her. Leave the body where it falls and then get back here."

"Yes, sir."

"And don't take liberties with her," said O'Neill. "If you do, we'll find out. We'll know what you did and we'll have to punish you."

"Yes, sir."

O'Neill looked at Becker. "Anything you want to say."

"No, sir. Except good luck."

"Thank you, sir," Henriks said.

"You go now. Report to me as soon as you've finished. If you're back by midnight, then you can join the assault force, but don't rush."

"Yes, sir." Henriks waited a moment and when neither O'Neill nor Becker spoke, he strolled off, more or less in the direction taken by Starling.

When he was out of earshot, Becker said, "You think that was a good idea?"

"I think that we had no choice. She's dangerous. The only thing we can do now is kill her. We'll blame it on the enemy. That'll anger the colonial office and strengthen our case against the locals."

"I suppose."

O'Neill looked up at the sun. "We've got about two hours of

daylight left. Get some more scouts out and get everyone fed.
We'll move into position for the attack after dark."

"Yes, sir."

Henriks walked to the rear of the column where a couple of the
ATVs were parked in the shade of a gigantic tree. The crews of
both of them sat on the ground, one of them holding a canteen
in his hand. His face was wet, as was the collar of his shirt.
None of the men had any rank insignia drawn on their
coveralls.

"Need to take the ATV," said Henriks.

"Says who?"

"Colonel."

One of the men stood up. He looked about half the size of
Henriks. He cradled a bolt-action hunting rifle in his arms. "I
can check."

Henriks pointed at his hat. "I'm a sergeant and I'm taking
one of the ATVs."

"You bring it back here."

"Yes."

"Keys are in them. Careful with them. We paid for them
ourselves."

Henriks climbed behind the wheel, settled himself in, and
then waited. He watched the column, and finally saw Starling
in another ATV pull away. He let her pass him, started his
vehicle, and took off after her.

She didn't seem to notice that he was back there. She never
turned around, and she didn't speed up. She drove to the south,
following the path created by the column as it had moved
forward. She came to the ford in a river, stopped there, and got
out to inspect the water.

Henriks pulled up beside her ATV, stopped his, and lifted
himself out. He walked down the bank to where she stood,
hands on her hips, surveying the river. She heard him coming,
jumped slightly and then turned to look. She grinned when she
recognized him.

"Looks deeper than it was earlier," she said.

Henriks studied her carefully. She was good-looking with
short brown hair and brown eyes. Even the scar didn't detract
from her looks.

"You think it's deeper?" she asked.

Henriks shook his head. "No reason for it to be deeper. Looks about the same."

"Then the ATV should be able to ford it again." She glanced over his shoulder nervously as if searching for more of the army approaching. "You want something?"

"Colonel sent me back to take care of you."

She relaxed, misunderstanding him. "That was kind of him."

"Yes, I suppose so."

She turned to look at the water again. Henriks stopped short, behind her, studying her body. A little stocky, but still good. Too bad to waste it, but the Colonel's orders had been very clear.

He raised his shotgun, thumbed back the hammer with an audible metallic click and waited. When she started to turn again, he pulled the trigger.

The blast caught her in the side and lifted her from her feet. Blood exploded from her, bathing her side and chest. Her head snapped back as she fell into the water. She groaned once, tried to lift herself up, out of the shallow water. She didn't make it, falling back into the river. Her blood spread out around her, turning the water crimson.

Henriks stepped to the body, looked down at the face. It was a waxy white but there was no wound on it. Just the gaping hole in her side showing a lung and white bone. Her eyes were open, unseeing, and water was filling her mouth rapidly.

"Sorry," he said. He then turned, walked to the ATV and put his shotgun into the rear. He searched her vehicle, throwing her gear out, on the ground, stomping on some of it, kicking some of it, and tossing the rest into the river.

Finished, he climbed into his own ATV, backed, and turned, driving away. He didn't look back at the body of the woman. He felt nothing about the act. His colonel had ordered it and that was good enough for him.

As the sun disappeared, O'Neill, his scouts, and two or three others began the slow climb up the ridge line. They leaned into the task, ignoring the dust they were kicking up. With the sun nearly gone, it wasn't as hot as it had been during the middle of the afternoon.

As they approached the crest, O'Neill held up a hand and

then bent at the waist, walked a few more feet and then got down on his belly. He turned his attention on the others, who were spread out around him.

He whispered his orders. "Let's keep it quiet from here on."

He worked his way higher and higher until he reached the crest of the hill. He slipped over it, and in the shadows below him was the enemy camp. Not the mud huts of the village at the river, but a real camp. Tents and fires. Nothing of a permanent nature down there. He counted, lost track, and started again.

The scout had been right. No more than fifty individuals down there, about half of them adult males. They'd have to kill them or worry about them coming up from behind when the attack on the mass camp started.

"You seen enough?" he asked Becker quietly.

Becker nodded and then pointed to the right. O'Neill saw it too. The enemy'd taken the precaution of posting a guard. If there was one, there were probably others. O'Neill used his binoculars, saw two more and was satisfied. The innocent didn't post guards. Military units posted guards. That confirmed it to his satisfaction.

He pushed himself to the rear, backing up carefully as he watched the enemy camp. When it slipped from sight, he stood, hunched over, and hurried fifteen or twenty feet down the slope. Satisfied that they couldn't see him, he stood upright.

"Anyone see anything unusual about that camp?" he asked, his voice low.

Becker was the only one to speak. "No, sir."

"Good. We'll have our scouts take out the guards and then hit them from this side, chasing them out. That open field will make a good killing ground. We should be able to run the survivors to ground from the ATVs."

"No blocking force?" asked Becker.

"I don't think we'll need it. Just designate a platoon to sweep through shooting everything right and left but to keep going. Once they're on the far side, they can turn and form for the blocking force."

"We going to use the ATVs?" asked Becker. "They'll make noise climbing the hill."

"Not that much. We'll form a skirmish line up here as the

vehicles are brought up. If the enemy hears us, the skirmishers will have to pin them down."

"We go at midnight?" asked Becker.

"We go at midnight."

From his perch at the top of the ridge line, O'Neill could see nothing. The moon was behind them so that the enemy camp was in the shadows created by the hill. The starlight didn't penetrate the light cloud cover. It was the moon that bothered him. It would illuminate them during the attack. He'd forgotten about the damn moon.

"Scouts have been moving for about thirty minutes," whispered Becker.

"We'll give them another fifteen. Then we commence the assault."

"The vehicles?"

O'Neill pulled at his lips. He suddenly felt hot, though the heat of the day had broken as the sun had set. "One at a time, you start them. Watch me. You see a light up here, you shut everything down."

"Yes, sir." Becker slipped to the rear and disappeared into the darkness. A moment later, down the slope, he stood, visible in the moonlight.

"Damn," said O'Neill.

He kept his eyes on his watch. He ignored the line of men and women on either side of him. He ignored the quiet rustling as they shifted their positions. They weren't making enough noise to alert the enemy. The light breeze was stirring the grasses around them. That covered any noise they made.

Straining his ears, he could make out the sound of an ATV starting, but once the engine caught, the noise disappeared. After five minutes, he figured that all of them must have been started. He could detect no sound from them, but then the ground at the foot of the slope began to shimmer and squirm and he realized that it was the motion of the ATVs. He still couldn't hear them.

"It's going to work," he said quietly. He turned and used his binoculars. There was a dim flickering as the last of the campfires burned low. The enemy was asleep, figuring that it was safe.

The only sound he heard was the rustling as the ATVs

crushed the grass. The engine noises were well muffled. They'd never hear them coming.

O'Neill pushed himself to the rear and then stood. He climbed into the front seat of the ATV. He lifted his rifle, worked the bolt to make sure that a round was chambered. He touched the safety, flicked it on, and then looked at the line of vehicles idling just below the crest of the hill. On the military crest, ten feet from the top.

O'Neill stood and lifted his right hand into the air like a wagon master at the head of a train. He waved it forward and dropped back into the seat. The ATV lurched forward, crested the hill, and began the run down on the enemy village.

The soldiers around him began to cheer. They shouted as the ATVs picked up speed. There was a single shot and then a rippling of fire. O'Neill wished the men had waited, but now they were close enough it probably didn't matter.

As the angle changed, he could make out shapes. Two were up and running at the attackers. O'Neill lowered his rifle and fired, but the ATV was bouncing on the rough terrain. The shot was wild.

"Halt," ordered O'Neill suddenly. He slapped at his own driver and screamed, "Halt."

His vehicle slowed and then stopped. O'Neill leaped over the side, knelt and opened fire. He didn't bother with the iron sights on the rifle. He looked over the top of the barrel, aimed at the closest figure and shot. There was a wet slap, a shriek of pain, and the creature fell.

Other ATVs were slowing. Men and women were jumping out. Some were rushing forward while others held their positions, firing at the shapes of the enemy. The attack came from the left. A dozen of the males screaming as they swarmed up the slope toward the humans.

O'Neill turned to meet that threat. He fired, worked the bolt, and fired again, but missed both times. He kept at it until his rifle was empty. The enemy kept on coming, ignoring the firing of the humans. One of them raised its giant club and brought it down with a grunt and the sound of a ripe melon hitting concrete.

"Oh my God," said someone, the voice filled with panic.

Two of the humans turned to run, fleeing back up the slope.

O'Neill ignored them. He tossed his rifle into the rear of the ATV and drew his pistol.

"Take them now," he said.

"Got three coming up here."

O'Neill glanced down the slope but couldn't see much there. Someone had kicked out the last of the fires. There were black shapes moving but he didn't know which were his soldiers and which were the enemy.

"Pick your targets," he said. "Alpha company, to the right. Stop them on the right."

"Got them," yelled a voice.

"Here they come again."

O'Neill saw a bunch of shapes rushing up the hill at them. For an instant he was afraid that it was his own men and then realized that they wouldn't be running toward the ATVs.

"Cut them down."

There was a rattling of fire from the rifles and then the twin boom boom of a shotgun. One of the creatures was lifted from his feet and cartwheeled away.

O'Neill fired his pistol at the threat. He pulled the trigger until it was empty and then he stood, leaping to the rear. Crouched behind his ATV, he reloaded the pistol, holstered it, and then grabbed his rifle. When he had it loaded, he stood, but there was no movement on the slope. Farther down there was firing. The muzzle flashes twinkled like fireflies on a summer afternoon.

"Let's go," he shouted. He started down the hill, walking at first, but picking up speed until he was running. The men and women around him joined him. Those of the skirmish line left behind on the crest suddenly screamed and they began running down the hill too.

The tide swept into the campsite. O'Neill saw a wounded creature in front of him. O'Neill kicked it in the head and then fired at its torso. The round slammed home and the creature died without a sound.

They moved through the camp shooting at anything that moved, but the firing was now sporadic. The soldiers had penetrated all areas and had flushed all the locals. They chased a few toward the perimeter, shooting them as they fled. O'Neill followed a group of them checking the hiding places, shooting at the bodies of the locals that were scattered through the remains of the camp.

Finished with that, and with the shooting having faded to single shots, O'Neill stopped and looked back. On the slope behind him he could see the line of parked ATVs and the bodies of those killed.

Becker ran up to him. "I think that's got it."

"I want security out now. And I want those ATVs brought down. Lights on."

"Lights on?"

"Right. I want to see what we have here. Then I want a thorough search to make sure that no one has escaped."

"Yes, sir."

O'Neill recognized Pruggs. "First Sergeant, I want a casualty count."

"Yes, sir. We've four dead so far."

"I don't want a partial. You report to me when you have accurate numbers."

"Yes, sir."

Jones rolled up in an ATV. He slid to a halt and then vaulted over the side. Grinning, he said, "We have secured the enemy camp."

"Very good. Let's make sure of that."

"Yes, sir."

There was no mistaking the enthusiasm in his voice. O'Neill stood for a moment. It had been a repeat of the last attack, only this time he'd lost a few men and women.

"Ah, hell," he said, knowing that it had been a good fight.

16

FLAGSHIP OF THE TENTH INTERPLANETARY INFANTRY REGIMENT

GARVEY WAS SURE that the ship's doctor would be able to answer his questions. He knew that he could call up some of the information on the ship's computers if he wanted, but Garvey preferred talking to living humans. He could ask questions that a computer might not understand but that a human could interpret for him. He didn't have to think of half a dozen ways to ask the question so that the computer would be able to find the data he wanted.

Garvey had never been to the ship's sick bay. Before he'd launched into space, he'd been seen by an Earth doctor, and on the shuttle, as the first wave of nausea swept over him, he'd been treated. But once he'd arrived on the flagship, he had never had a reason to see the doctor.

The sick bay surprised him somewhat. He'd thought he'd find something of a cross between an emergency room on Earth and a laboratory. What he actually found was a pleasant office in muted colors and soft tones. There was carpeting on the deck, paneling on the bulkheads, a holo window of the space outside, and a number of chairs arranged in a conversation pit. It was a relaxing atmosphere.

A hatch to the right opened and a man appeared. He wore a white smock and held a towel in his hands, drying them. "Can I help you?"

"I'd like to talk to a doctor," said Garvey.

"Well, I'm a flight surgeon. That help?"

"I don't know. Do you have a few minutes?"

The flight surgeon turned, tossed the towel back into the other cabin, and then came forward. He gestured at the conversation pit. "Let's sit down . . ."

"Garvey. I'm the reporter assigned to the Tenth."

"Maybe I'd better not talk to you. Reporters tend to hear what they want to hear." He was grinning broadly.

"Doctor?"

"Clodomeyer. Robert Clodomeyer."

"Doctor Clodomeyer. Some strange things going on here."

"Not that I'm aware of," said Clodomeyer. He was still grinning. "But what the layman thinks is strange is often good medical procedure."

Garvey nodded and grinned back. He wanted to discuss that a little to put Clodomeyer at ease, but he didn't know that much about the medical procedures on the ship. Finally, because he couldn't think of any other questions, he asked, "What can you tell me about cloning?"

"It's the creation of a genetically identical organism from a single individual through asexual methods."

"You take the genetic material from one organism and create a whole new organism," said Garvey.

"Exactly. You don't need much in the way of genetic material either. As long as the RNA and DNA are intact, the material from a single cellular source is sufficient. The genetic code of the entire individual is contained in each cell."

"The technique is common?" asked Garvey.

Clodomeyer shrugged. "What's common? The techniques for cloning have been around for decades. Most . . . not necessarily most, but a wide variety of fruit and nut trees and ornamental plants are essentially clones. The techniques for reproducing animals were demonstrated in the last half of the twentieth century."

"So you're not surprised by cloning?"

"Why should I be? Techniques for cloning of the higher animals has only recently been accomplished and the first human was cloned about a decade ago. There are ethical questions that should be addressed but science often runs in advance of morality and ethics."

"Scientists worry about ethics?" asked Garvey.

Clodomeyer stared at the reporter. "I don't know if I should be insulted by that question or not. Scientists often wonder what will be done with their discoveries. Most scientists have a well-developed sense of ethics, but those who exploit the discoveries are often less than ethical. That's where the problems come in."

"Have you done any work in cloning?"

"Me? No. I was more interested in preventive medicine. Research holds no fascination for me."

"Cloning of humans is possible?"

"Of course. Once the techniques are understood, it is simply a matter of creating the environment in which the clone can be actively grown. That's not an easy task. The lower the organism is on the evolutionary scale, the easier it is. But the techniques apply throughout."

"You'd have no problems?" said Garvey.

"Define problems. Cloning a human? I couldn't do it now, though I do understand the process. I'd have to learn a great deal more in that field before I would even attempt such an experiment."

Clodomeyer was quiet for a moment, lost in thought. Garvey realized that he smelled like a doctor. There was something slightly medicinal in the air. Clodomeyer, like most doctors, probably wore the disinfectants like some men wore cologne. He smelled like the interior of a hospital. Garvey wasn't sure that he liked it.

Clodomeyer broke into his thoughts. "Ethically, I would have some problems with it too. There are questions that I wouldn't want to have to answer."

"Such as?"

Clodomeyer scratched the back of his neck. "Now remember, I'm talking off the top of my head here, but one of the things that comes to mind is whether a cloned person is a real person."

"Meaning what?"

Again Clodomeyer hesitated. "Well, standard individuals are the result of a union between two people. Might be the result of in vitro fertilization, but it is still between two people. Those who are the result of a cloning are not. Does that make them less than human? I would say not, but there are those who look for any reason to feel superior to their fellows. Once it was the color of the skin or the color of the hair or just the person's background. This would be one area where I think the social dilemmas would be ripe for exploitation."

"I don't understand," said Garvey.

"Now I'm not saying this will happen, but there could be those who claim that a human made strictly in the laboratory, as a clone would be, is not really human and therefore open for all sorts of unpleasant exploitation. Slavery comes to mind. You can own the clone because it isn't a real person. It has not been endowed by the Creator."

"I can't see that," said Garvey.

"Think about it," said Clodomeyer. "You feel there has to be two of you to accomplish anything, so you head down to the lab to create another you. Do you own that creation? Is it property? What are it's legal rights?"

"I hadn't thought . . . but you could see it was a real, living being," said Garvey.

"Look at the debate over abortions that rocked the United States at the end of the twentieth century. You'd think the answer would be fairly cut and dried if you looked objectively at the facts, but it wasn't. Both sides made impassioned pleas. And that's the key. Passion. It wouldn't be viewed rationally."

"Then you're against it," said Garvey. He wondered why he asked the question.

"Nope. I said there were questions that should be answered before we begin to clone humans in any wholesale fashion."

Garvey nodded. "But the techniques exist?"

"Hell," said Clodomeyer. "You've seen that yourself."

Carter was monitoring the activity on the planet's surface with only half an eye. It was night where the majority of the people lived. That meant nothing to him. With the array of sensors and equipment available to him, he could see down onto the planet's surface as well as he could during the day. The only problem was that coverage was not complete, that he had to shift the eyes electronically and thus he couldn't receive input from the entire surface. He had to search for areas of interest before he could focus in for the specifics.

But the fire fight, when it erupted after midnight, stood out like a beacon. Carter immediately homed in on it, and began to record what he was seeing.

The firing was all one-sided. Rifles, pistols and shotguns. Infrared detected the heat of vehicle engines and was able to separate the humans from the locals based on the differences in body heat.

With long range radars and various sensors, combined with a computer projection of the territory and interpretation of the images, Carter was able to watch the battle like an old Indian chief standing on the hillside watching his warriors attack the army.

As the humans swept down on the few locals, Carter reached over and touched a button. "Colonel Jefferson, this is Carter in Intelligence."

There was a moment's delay and then, "Jefferson here."

"Sir, I've detected a battle going on down there."

"I'll be there in just a moment."

"Yes, sir."

Carter turned back to his console and tried to anticipate Jefferson's questions. The colonel would want to know exactly where the battle was fought, strength on both sides, and the distribution of Torrence's forces on the ground. He pulled a keyboard close and began to type.

Before he could finish, the door behind him hissed open and Jefferson entered. "Show me what you've got."

Without a word, Carter typed a command. The main screen changed and showed the battle.

"Real time or recorded?"

"This is the beginning of the tape," said Carter. "I don't have the beginning of the fight."

Jefferson glanced to the right and dragged a chair over. He dropped into it. "What's happening here?"

"Near as I can tell, the colonial militia located another band of the locals and have attacked them. No evidence that the locals have any firearms. A fairly one-sided fight."

"Locals did anything to provoke the attack?"

"I didn't see the beginning of it but my guess would be no. I've seen no evidence that the locals have exhibited much in the way of hostility."

"Where's Torrence?"

Carter grinned to himself and touched a button. Another

screen lighted, showing a map of the planet's surface. "Torrence is marked in blue, city is in yellow and the site of the battle is red."

Jefferson turned his attention back to the screen. "This still going on?"

The scene changed abruptly. The flashes of brightness that marked the firing of weapons was gone. Now shadowy shapes slipped over the field, looking at the bodies of those killed. Periodically there was a flash as someone shot a wounded creature.

"Taking no prisoners," said Carter.

Jefferson watched the real-time scene for a moment and then said, "There any concentrations of the locals around? Other concentrations?"

Carter used his keyboard again, the sound of his typing suddenly noisy. It was as if all other sound had been deadened by the scene shown.

"There's a large group of them here, about two hundred and fifty miles away."

"And the militia's been heading?" said Jefferson.

"In that direction. No question that the locals' camp is their ultimate destination."

"All right. We'd . . . I'd better get Major Torrence alerted. Let her go in to protect the locals. She can get there, surround them and keep the colonials away from them."

"That our job?" asked Carter. "Protecting the locals?"

"Our job," said Jefferson sharply, "is to keep the fighting from breaking out. At the moment it looks as if the guilty parties are the humans. Therefore we protect the locals and keep the humans away."

"Yes, sir."

"Give me hard copies of the maps including the terrain features, though Torrence has floaters. I want all villages, ours, theirs, and additional camps, plotted. Lines of communications for the locals and anything else that you think Major Torrence will need."

"Yes, sir."

Jefferson stood up and looked at the screen. The humans had finished shooting the wounded and were moving back, away from the smashed local camp. Two of their ATVs separated suddenly and began a run toward the closest colonial village.

"What's that?"

"I think they're evacuating the wounded," said Carter.

"Let's intercept them."

"To kill them?"

"Hell, no, Carter. What the hell are you thinking about? No. I want to treat the wounded. Get a shuttle to intercept and then have our sick bay care for them. A concession to the humans. We do good for both sides."

"I'll get a projection to the shuttle bay so that the intercept can be made."

"Good." Jefferson stood for a moment watching the screen. He shook his head. It was typical of the human race. Create a war where none existed. Humans had been doing it for centuries. Men and women had been killing men and women in the name of religion, manifest destiny, retribution, and for their own good since the human race had been able to think in abstract terms.

"Anything changes here, you get word to me immediately," ordered Jefferson.

"Of course, sir."

"Get the coordinates up to Captain Clemens on the bridge as soon as you have them. I'll alert the shuttle crew and the sick bay."

"Yes, sir."

Jefferson didn't want to leave then. He wanted to stay there to watch what was happening, but knew it would do no good. It was time to get the ball rolling. He had orders to issue to Torrence so that she could get started moving her battalion. The mission had been changed radically.

Just before he left, he asked, "What's the speed on those ATVs?"

"They've been averaging about twenty miles an hour as they moved in column. They could bump it up but I wouldn't expect them to travel faster than forty or fifty miles an hour. Besides, it doesn't look as if they're going to move on tonight."

"Then we have some time," said Jefferson. With that he left the intell office.

17

DELTA ROYAL THREE

JOHN, SIX ONE TWO, his platoon sergeant, and the squad leaders sat on the floor of their room. The cots had been pushed to one side, the chairs stacked out of the way, and the door had been shut. The assistant squad leaders had been left in charge of the platoon. John, Six One Two, had tried to impress upon them the responsibility of command. They had their chance to prove that they were worthy of the responsibility they held. They were not to disturb the squad leaders, the platoon sergeant, or the lieutenant unless the planet had suddenly burst into flame. It was their opportunity to shine.

When John, Six One Two, had entered the small room, the squad leaders had slowly come to attention. Sara, Six One Three, followed and then said, "Everyone. At ease."

One by one the squad leaders had sat down. John, Six One Two, was now unsure what to do. He was uncomfortable in the room, afraid to move or to speak, afraid that someone would misinterpret his actions. It seemed easier to sit there quietly, and let things happen. The problem was that nothing was happening.

Sara, Six One Three, stood near the door and then leaned back against it. She surveyed the others, her brothers and sisters, and could see their nervousness. "What is wrong here?" she asked.

Timothy, Seven One One, nodded toward the lieutenant. He opened his mouth to speak and then didn't.

"That is your brother," said Sara, Six One Three. "He is just like you."

"He is the lieutenant," said Lisa, Seven Four Five.

"He is your brother," said Sara, Six One Three. "Can we forget rank for a moment or two?"

"I can if he can," said Timothy, Seven One One. He glanced at the lieutenant. "But in all the time he has trained with us, he has always remained aloof. We have been reminded daily that John, Six One Two, is the lieutenant and must be treated with respect. His decisions are to be obeyed. All his orders are to be obeyed."

John, Six One Two, said, "There is a time-out. For the moment I am not the lieutenant and you all are not the senior NCOs. We are brothers and sisters."

"No," said Lisa, Seven Four Five. "That cannot be. You are the lieutenant." She had a look of horror on her face as if she had just learned that Santa Claus was unreal.

Sara, Six One Three, said, "None of you have worked as closely as I have with the lieutenant, but I know him. He is our brother."

Timothy, Seven One One, stood suddenly and then held out a hand as if formally welcoming a new man to the platoon. "I would be pleased if you'd join us, sir."

John, Six One Two, laughed. At that moment the formality of the room disintegrated and they were no longer lieutenant and senior NCOs. Now they were just brothers and sisters who hadn't been able to talk to one another in a long time.

Now, they sat on the floor, a deck of cards among them. Eric, Seven Two Three, was dealing. Shelia, Seven Four Eight, had lost several hands in a row and was naked. Eric, Seven Two Three, hadn't done much better and had retained only his shorts.

As Eric, Seven Two Three, completed dealing, John, Six One Two, who had a run of beginner's luck, asked, "What happens when everyone has lost everything."

Lisa, Seven Four Five, grinned broadly. "We just see what develops from that point."

John, Six One Two, nodded, but still didn't understand the purpose of the game. He'd seen each of them naked before.

There had been training exercises, showers, and a dozen other activities. But Lisa, Seven Four Five, seemed to be excited about the prospect of having the lieutenant lose all his clothes in a poker game.

"I'm afraid that I don't see the point of this," said John, Six One Two.

"You'll see," said Sara, Six One Three. "Some of your training has been less than adequate."

"We talked about that earlier," said John, Six One Two.

"About what?" asked Eric, Seven Two Three. He announced, "Five card draw poker. One-eyed jacks and the man with the ax are wild."

Shelia, Seven Four Eight, grinned broadly. "Now I get the cards," she said.

They completed the hand and Shelia, Seven Four Eight, held the winning cards, four threes, if the jack she held was counted. Sara, Six One Three, had the worst hand. She stood up, unhooked her jumpsuit and let it slide down, revealing her body. She kicked the garment away, turned slowly letting everyone get a good look at her even though she still wore panties.

"Your deal," said Lisa, Seven Four Five. She handed the cards to John, Six One Two.

He accepted them, shuffled, and then sat there for a moment looking at his brothers and sisters. For the first time he didn't feel completely alone. He reached to the right and put a hand on Lisa, Seven Four Five's knee. She put her hand over his.

"I don't think I've ever felt this good," said John, Six One Two.

"You're not afraid of losing your command authority because of fraternization with the enlisted pukes?" asked Timothy, Seven One One.

"That," said John, Six One Two, "is something that I'm beginning to realize is not true. A commander can form relationships with the troops in his command. Colonel Jefferson showed me that."

"How?"

"Just by the way he acted with the others." John, Six One Two, looked at the cards in his hand and then at his brothers and sisters. "There's a fine line that has to be walked. The commander must be able to command when necessary, but he must know when to do it. A commander must be able to relax with the troops to show that he is just like them. He has to do that to inspire confidence in them."

"And I sit here naked," said Shelia, Seven Four Eight.

"Because you're a lousy card player," said Eric, Seven Two Three. "Simple as that."

The knock at the door startled no one. Sara, Six One Three, tossed down the two cards that John, Six One Two, had finally dealt. "I told them we didn't want to be bothered." She opened the door and then said, "Major Torrence."

Torrence pushed her way into the room, looked at them sitting on the floor but said nothing about it. Instead, she said, "We've got orders."

John, Six One Two, was suddenly embarrassed. He stood up, stepped in front of Shelia, Seven Four Eight, as if that could hide the fact that she was completely naked.

"We're ready, ma'am."

Torrence laughed. "I would suggest that you all get back into uniform. Then, get the platoon ready to move out. We've got about thirty minutes."

"Yes, ma'am."

Torrence closed the door as she left. John, Six One Two, stood and looked back. His face was bright red and he looked as if he'd been caught with a hand in the cookie jar.

"Don't worry about it," said Sara, Six One Three. "If she'd been annoyed, she would have said something right then."

John, Six One Two, said, "Of course. I guess the game is over. We'll have to do it again sometime."

"Of course," said Shelia, Seven Four Eight.

"I'll meet you all in the squad bay in about fifteen minutes."

"Yes, sir," said Sara, Six One Three. "Everything will be fine."

John, Six One Two, nodded, but he didn't believe it. He knew that Torrence would never say anything to him in front of his senior NCOs. She'd wait until they were alone and then she'd read him the riot act. That was how it was done.

It didn't take thirty minutes to get the battalion assembled and ready to move. Torrence had to decide who was going to take which assignment. She had to decide who would move first and who would hang back. And she had to decide how much information to give Clovers, who would in turn report to Nast. There were things that she didn't want Nast to know.

She stood to one side of the open field, in the humidity of the very early morning. Dew was forming on some surfaces. It was sticky and uncomfortable and she wished that they were inside, even without air-conditioning.

"Floaters are inspected, fueled, and ready," said an NCO, who came close and saluted.

"Thank you." Torrence turned to Martuesi. "Load your company."

"Yes, ma'am."

"I want you to land ten klicks to the west of the major local camp. Stay out of their sight. String out there. Platoon formation. Everyone stay in radio communication with everyone else."

"Yes, ma'am."

"You have questions, you call."

"Understood."

Torrence held out a hand. "Good luck."

"Just one question. Rules of engagement."

"I don't think the locals will present a problem. Your force is large enough to frighten them away."

"I wasn't concerned with the locals. It's that damned colonial militia."

Without a hesitation, Torrence said, "You return fire for fire received. You run into any of them, you disarm them and send them home."

"Their weapons are privately owned."

"They'll be returned when the current mess is solved. Until then, we don't need an armed force roaming the countryside," said Torrence.

"Yes, ma'am." She saluted and trotted off to organize her company.

Torrence walked across the grass and found John, Six One Two, standing with two of his NCOs. Torrence returned their salutes. "I'm going to use you as scouts. Throw you out along the line of march of the militia. I want them under observation by our people. I want them to know that we've got them under observation."

"Yes, ma'am," said John, Six One Two.

"You are not to engage them. We'll have our battalion to

separate them from the locals. Your job is simply to keep them under surveillance so that they know they're under surveillance."

"If they fire on us?"

"You fire back," said Torrence. "But you disengage immediately. I don't want two groups of humans fighting one another. If you have trouble, you call for help. We'll have the battalion there in minutes to back you up."

"Yes, ma'am."

"Questions?"

"No," said John, Six One Two.

"Floaters will be available in about thirty minutes. You'll have the use of them for as long as you need them. Maps will be provided. Stay in radio contact."

"Yes, ma'am."

Torrence wanted to say more. She wanted to say something about the traditions of the Tenth, but there were no real traditions to speak of. She wanted to say something about duty, but the lieutenant and his NCOs were aware of that. The problem, she realized, is that she didn't trust them completely because she'd never seen them in combat. In training they had been competent, but training was training and combat was a different game. Some just couldn't handle it.

Finally, realizing that they would either succeed or fail and that nothing she said would change that now, she said, "Good luck."

"Thank you, ma'am."

She left them standing there and returned to the main body of the battalion. The men and women stood in a ragged formation waiting for their instructions. No one seemed overly concerned now. It wasn't as if they were dropping into combat or into the unknown of some planet still being surveyed. They were going in to separate the humans from the locals and if someone got killed, the most likely candidates were the colonists. No large armed enemy force.

Torrence walked among the officers and tried to listen in without anyone realizing it. She got snatches of conversation. They all figured it would be a cakewalk. No reason for anyone to get hurt and if the humans caused too many troubles, there was fleet targeting to use lasers, bombs, or missiles from orbit.

A few minutes of that and anyone on the planet would be ready to surrender.

That sort of talk frightened Torrence because troops could get overconfident and then get killed. But she couldn't say anything without undermining the authority of the officers and then making the enlisted troops nervous. At the moment, there was no reason to suspect the worst. It was a situation that demanded restraint and little else.

She found Martuesi standing in front of her assembled company. "You ready?"

"Yes, ma'am."

"Then have your first platoon board the floaters."

Martuesi turned and called. "Platoon leaders, take charge of your platoons and prepare to board the floaters. First platoon, move out."

The platoon leaders saluted individually. Martuesi lifted her hand to her forehead, spun in a semicircle and returned all the salutes at once. First platoon broke into squads and marched toward the first four of the floaters.

To Martuesi, she said, "Don't let the troops get careless. I don't want anyone killed because we were careless. The difference is that we can talk to the humans and we outgun the locals."

"Understood."

Torrence watched as the first squad of the first platoon boarded the floaters. Everything was moving smoothly, but she had a feathery feeling in her stomach. It was the old military adage that if something hadn't gone wrong, it was about to. She just didn't know what it could be.

18

DELTA ROYAL THREE

O'NEILL WALKED UP and down the line of ATVs, looking at the men and women sitting in them. They had cleaned up after the battle, sending the wounded off for medical treatment, and burying the twelve dead humans. O'Neill had momentarily thought about taking the bodies back to the colonial headquarters, but knew it wouldn't happen. No need for it.

He looked up at the moon and at the stars now barely visible through the thin overcast and wondered about the time. On Earth he might have been able to figure it out, but he hadn't been on the planet long enough to understand the cycle of the moons and stars there. He couldn't tell them apart most of the time.

"We going to pull out now?" asked Becker.

"Let's retreat to the top of the hill and camp there for the rest of the night," said O'Neill.

"Got a long ways to go tomorrow," said Becker. "Be easier if we started now."

"There's nothing difficult about riding in an ATV for a couple of hours," said O'Neill. "We'll leave at first light."

"Scouts?"

"Let them have a couple of hours of sleep and then send them out, though Starling provided us with good information about the main body of the enemy."

"Tomorrow's really going to end it?" asked Becker.

O'Neill shrugged and realized that Becker probably wouldn't be able to see it in the dark. He said, "I don't know. Tomorrow we'll hit the largest assembly of the enemy we know of. Word will get back to the others. They'll be so busy looking over their shoulders that they should never bother us again."

"Seems to me that on Earth the American Indians broke up into smaller groups to hit the army."

"No," said O'Neill. "They broke into small groups to get away. That was the end of them. Tomorrow could end it completely for us."

"Yes, sir."

O'Neill raised his voice. "Drivers, let's get the vehicles up to the hilltop. Form a loose circle up there."

A couple of starters whined. The headlights popped on now that there was no reason for secrecy. The only enemy around were dead.

O'Neill watched them turn and then bounce back up the hill. One or two of them, and then more and more until the last of them was on the move. The dust rose and drifted down at him, a gray cloud nearly invisible in the starlight. For a moment it masked the odor of death that hung over the battlefield.

O'Neill had thought that the odor of death was a cliche used in bad books but now knew it wasn't true. Blood smelled of hot copper and when a human died there was an odor of bowel, a stench that was worse than an overused outhouse on a hot afternoon. That was the odor of death and that was what he smelled on that field.

He started to walk up the slope, realizing that he should never have remained behind like that. No telling what could happen to a lone human. But his soldiers were only a hundred yards away, at the top of the hill. The enemy couldn't get at him.

As he approached the circle, he could hear the party in full swing. They had parked the ATVs as he had ordered, but had pointed them in and left the lights on. Someone had scraped together enough wood for a bonfire. Men and women were dancing to music blaring from the tape players and radios that had been turned off all day. It was a riot of sound that mixed together into something that was nearly pleasing. O'Neill wondered if it was just the fact they could now make noise without a worry of retribution.

He stopped behind one of the ATVs and watched the dancers. It was as confusing as hand-to-hand combat. One man spun a woman around so hard that she stumbled, falling to her face. Others roared with laughter.

A lone women danced near the bonfire and began a slow strip, tossing her clothing into the flames. She kept going until she was completely nude, glanced at the people watching, and then kept on dancing, unconcerned.

A man appeared with a bottle in his hand. He gave it to a friend who drank from it. They began passing it around until it was empty. It too flew into the fire.

O'Neill stepped out of the shadows. Those closest to him, who recognized him, froze, waiting to see what he would say or do. When he folded his arms across his chest and leaned back against the ATV, they cheered wildly and ran to join the dancers.

"You going to let it go?" asked Becker.

"No way to stop it now. In the first few minutes we could've but not now. We've got to let it burn out or we'll lose the cohesiveness that was created during the fight."

"I'm sorry," said Becker.

"Don't be. I might not have stopped it either. Who knows? It's going to set our plans back by a couple of hours but that's all. This can't last long. They're working too hard at it, drinking too fast."

"That's another thing," said Becker. "Where in the hell did they get those bottles?"

"Armies always find alcohol. Soldiers always have bottles. Better to let them drink it now than to have to confiscate it later."

A woman staggered up, threw her arms around O'Neill and kissed him on the lips. O'Neill leaned back, tried to avoid her lips and failed. She stuck her tongue in his mouth and then dropped her left hand to feel his crotch. Becker pulled her off him.

"HEY!" she shouted.

O'Neill blocked her. "I'll just watch for a while."

"Suit yourself," she said. "But you don't know what you're missing. I was ready."

"I could see that," said O'Neill as the woman spun back into the mass. He then leaned close to Becker. "Let it go another hour and then quietly, and I mean quietly, move among them and suggest they need their rest."

"Yes, sir. Where will you be?"

O'Neill shrugged. "Trying to get some rest myself."

Torrence used the recon floater to inspect the entire area, including the placement of Martuesi's company, the locals' camp, and then her own unit. She wanted to make sure that the placement was right and, given the lay of the land, and the direction to O'Neill's militia, she was sure that either she or Martuesi was in a position to intercept.

They changed course and flew back to her own lines. The platoons of the company were strung out over nearly a dozen klicks. A thin line to inhibit the assault should it come. With floaters, assistance wasn't that far away.

As it touched down, Torrence climbed out. One of the NCOs came up. "We're on half alert now. Figured on letting the troops catch a little shut-eye."

"I don't have a problem with that as long as someone makes sure that we don't slip to a third alert."

"Yes, ma'am."

"You get the command center established?"

"Over there, in that clump of trees. Antennas are up and comm-link with the fleet's established. Channel is open and someone is monitoring."

"Carter give you anything new?"

"Said that the militia has withdrawn from the battlefield and apparently is celebrating the victory."

Torrence stared at the man. He wasn't much more than a blank face in the dark. She could smell his breath and his body and wondered how he had gotten so dirty so fast.

"You sure about that?"

"Captain Carter said it. He's got the scanners to tell."

"Okay. Go to a quarter alert. They're not going to be moving on us tonight. Let's keep the troops rested as long as possible on this."

"Yes, ma'am."

She left him standing there and walked toward the clump of trees. As she approached, she was aware that eyes were on her.

She knew that she was being watched, but couldn't spot the sentry. The sentry was smart enough to recognize her from a distance and, if he or she didn't, was smart enough not to announce it to the world.

She found the small molded plastic cube that housed the communications equipment. It was a self-contained unit, large enough for two people. It held the radios, up-link to the computers, video, and a small microcomputer.

"You got anything?" Torrence asked the RTO.

"No, ma'am," she said. "Comm is established with the fleet and with Martuesi. Lieutenant Smith has checked in too."

For a moment she couldn't remember who Lieutenant Smith was and then realized he was the lieutenant of the special platoon. She had thought of him as the clone lieutenant when she thought of him at all.

"Anything from him?"

"No, ma'am. He's got his people spread out and is waiting for daylight to begin official operations."

"Thanks," said Torrence. She stepped back, out of the comm cube and grinned up at the night. Smith had been so embarrassed when she'd found him with the NCOs that it was funny. He was just beginning to unwind a little, get in with the troops and learn to see things from their perspective. It was about time.

The only thing she couldn't figure out was what in the hell they had been doing. It looked like a game of strip poker but that only worked with kids and people who didn't live in close contact with one another. What was the thrill about seeing someone naked that you'd seen in the shower that morning.

She shrugged, thought about it, and then decided that maybe it wasn't such a dumb idea. She wasn't sure if an officer should be playing that game with his NCOs, but then, if it wasn't that, it would have been something else. As long as he didn't force it, there wasn't a problem.

She moved through the trees and stopped at the edge of the clump. Looking up, she could see a bright star field. A band of brightness that crossed the sky near the northern horizon. A densely packed field that was brighter than anything she had seen on Earth.

She let her attention wander and then looked down, at the

ground. There was a company of infantry out there but she couldn't spot them. The men and women had done a good job of digging in and disguising their position.

There was nothing she could do at the moment except wait. See if the militia was going to move toward the locals or retreat to the city. Maybe the earlier victory would be enough for them. Somehow she didn't think it would be.

Garvey lay on his cot staring up at the ceiling. Something had been bothering him for the last few hours and he didn't have a clue as to what it was. Someone had said something that had raised the red flags but he couldn't see what they were flying over. He'd replayed the conversations and his activities in his mind, hoping for a clue, but nothing came.

At first he believed it was because he'd avoided the opportunity to land with the special battalion. A story could be found there. Anytime an armed force landed, there would be a story, even if it only told of the landing.

But he knew that hadn't been the problem. The real story was still on the ship, if he could figure it out. Laying there, staring up at the off-white overhead wasn't the way to find it. Concentrating on the problem had not solved it. Now it was time to circulate, find a few people and see if avoiding it would bring it to the surface.

Garvey got up and left his cabin. He prowled the corridors looking for someone to talk to. He hoped to find one of the female officers of either the battalion or the ship's company who wouldn't mind spending a little time with him, but they all seemed to have disappeared.

He found himself in the observation port looking out into the jet black of space sprinkled heavily with stars. To one side was a planet, several million miles away. If he stared, he could almost make out the disc. It was a brighter object than the stars far beyond it.

He felt another presence there and turned. Silvia James, an ensign whom he'd met once, stood behind him. She was tall, slender, and had long silver hair. She was one of the youngest officers assigned to the ship and Garvey had never said more than half a dozen words to her.

"I sometimes come here because it is so inspiring," she said.

Inspiring wasn't the word that Garvey would use. It was

frightening. Seeing all that, seeing the universe that stretched forever in all directions. When he thought about that, it frightened him. He could not conceive of the infinite. There had to be a beginning and an end, but there was no sign of it. Each advance made by the human race stretched the limits farther. The only limitation was the ability of humans to see. The boundaries of the universe might be ten billion light years today, but as technology increased, they would move to twelve billion or twenty billion and there was more beyond that.

When he didn't speak, she asked, "Don't you find it inspiring?"

"No," he said and let the thought die right there. He didn't want to get into a discussion of philosophies that would go nowhere except to keep him awake at night, frightened by them.

She moved forward and stood with him, shoulder to shoulder, almost touching him. "I don't know how you can avoid being inspired by it. So vast and so beautiful."

Garvey hesitated and then said, "Maybe because it is so vast and so beautiful."

"I suppose," she said. She glanced at him. "I don't find many people up here. I think the view frightens them."

Garvey felt his stomach flip over as he wondered if she could read minds. "In a way it is frightening."

"Yes. I suppose." She reached out to touch the thick glass in the windows. It looked as if she was trying to touch the stars themselves.

"It makes one feel insignificant," said Garvey, wondering why he was even talking about it. The smartest move was to remain quiet. A reporter learned that early on. Keep your mouth shut and let the subject talk.

"No," she said. "Not insignificant. Important, because you exist here. Insignificant is to never have lived."

Garvey didn't want to follow that path. Not with the talk of cloning humans still bouncing around his mind. Too many philosophical questions could drive a reporter crazy. Report the facts and don't worry about the interpretations put on all those facts.

She turned to face him, looking up into his face. "You're the reporter, aren't you?"

"Yes."

"I wonder why you bother."

That took Garvey by surprise. He stared at her. A young face unmarked by the sun, age, or gravity. An almost innocent face, framed by a mane of silver hair. "Bother about what?"

"You poke into places people don't want you to poke. You file stories people don't want told for people who don't want to hear them and then talk about the people's right to know," she said. It wasn't an accusation, exactly.

For an instant the anger flared in him as hot as a supernova and then it burned itself out completely. Instead of anger, he laughed and said, "It's a dirty job but someone has to do it."

"Why?" she asked.

"Because once in a while the story is important and it changes things for the better. Most of the time the people don't want to know. Sticking a camera in the face of a woman whose only child has just died to ask how she feels is not reporting. It is the question asked by the stupid and the unimaginative. But finding out why that child died. Not how, but why. Sometimes that does some good and keeps other mothers from losing their children."

She thought about that for a moment and then nodded. "Fair enough. Can I buy you a drink?"

Garvey made a production out of looking at his watch and then said, "I have a few free minutes."

He followed her out into the corridor wondering just what was going to happen. Maybe it would be only a drink or maybe two or maybe something more. At the moment he didn't know what he wanted to happen but he knew he wanted to have another human to talk to. As they reached the stern-lift, the earlier conversations he'd had suddenly exploded in his mind and he knew what he had been missing before. He knew the answer.

Suddenly, without thinking, he said, "Oh my God."

"What?"

"I have to see Colonel Jefferson immediately. He doesn't understand."

"What?"

"Come along," said Garvey grabbing her hand and tugging her into the stern-lift. "We've got to hurry."

19

DELTA ROYAL THREE

THE HORIZON WAS beginning to turn pink and the stars were just starting to fade. John, Six One Two, stood on the hilltop and watched as the shadows shifted and spread, and the tallest of the objects below him began to glow in the morning sun. Somewhere to the east of him was the militia. Six or seven hundred civilians who viewed themselves as soldiers. Men and women with no military training who thought that a warrior was merely a person with a gun.

Sara, Six One Three, approached from the dark side of the hill. She stopped near him and followed his gaze out. She didn't say anything to him. She just reached out and took his left hand in her right.

Without looking, John, Six One Two, said, "The major isn't going to forget."

"That still bothering you?" Sara, Six One Three, laughed. "She probably doesn't remember it."

"No. She remembers. Why do you think we got this assignment? It's the least important one. She knows that she can't trust us. Or rather, trust me."

"You said that you saw her and Colonel Jefferson."

John, Six One Two, pulled his hand free and looked at his sister. "Don't you see the difference? They're both officers. I was in with the enlisted troops."

"You were with your chain of command. It's the same thing," she said.

"No. Not at all. She's going to report it to the colonel and I'm going to be in trouble. I know it. You haven't had the same training that I have."

"You're worrying over nothing."

"I'm not. I knew that you couldn't understand. Now I've got to do something to redeem myself. If I don't, I'm going to be in real trouble."

"What could they do?"

John, Six One Two, shrugged helplessly. "I don't know. Remove me and put you in charge."

"I could handle it," she said.

"That's not the point. If they make that move, what happens to me?"

"You'd stay with the platoon in another capacity," said Sara, Six One Three.

"No. They'd take me away from it. You can't let the former commander, now as the lowest-ranking enlisted member, remain behind. Too many opportunities for trouble. I'll be sent away."

"They wouldn't do that," said Sara, Six One Three.

"Everything in the command structure manuals I've seen say they will. It's SOP."

"But . . . " she let the thought trail off.

"They don't understand that either." He moved closer to his sister so that he could feel the warmth of her body. "They don't understand anything about us. They think we're like the rest of humanity. They think that we could be sent out one by one to live a life of our own. They refuse to understand anything about us and now they're going to send me away. Just because I let myself have . . . let myself be talked into a game with you and the senior NCOs."

"We can't let that happen." She put an arm around his shoulders.

"There are ways," said John, Six One Two. "Military thought is fairly standard in some areas. They don't like the rogue, the maverick, though a successful maverick can get away with much. George Patton wasn't a standard general, but because he was such a great general, he could recover from the near-fatal mistakes he made."

"Yes," said Sara, Six One Three. She thought of Patton slapping a soldier and telling a group of journalists that the United States and Great Britain should rule the world after War

Two. World opinion had turned against him, but he was still allowed to command other units because he was a great general.

"Do you have a plan?" she asked him.

"I have been thinking about that. As the scout unit, we are to locate and watch the colonial militia. A job that anyone could do. But, if we could prevent it from attacking the locals, then we would receive recognition for our abilities. My mistake with the NCOs would be overlooked and ignored. No one remembers the last mistake when the current battle is fought."

"Are you planning to attack them?" asked Sara, Six One Three.

"No. Just stop them and turn them. Prevent the battle. Send them home and we will win great favor." He hesitated and then asked, "Do you think it will work?"

"Major Torrence has her battalion protecting the locals," said Sara, Six One Three.

John, Six One Two, nodded his understanding. The real enemy of the conflict was not the locals but the militia. They were out of control. They were roaming the countryside attacking and killing innocents. They were keeping the conflict alive in their minds and with their actions.

"We must find them and turn them around," said John, Six One Two. "They are little more than an armed rabble. Certainly no match for a well-trained, well-equipped platoon."

"You think this is a good idea?" asked Sara, Six One Three, quietly.

"It's the only thing I can think of. The only way to make the Major forget what she saw."

"All right then," said Sara, Six One Three. "I'll alert the squad leaders. When do you want to move out?"

"As soon as the sun is up. I want to intercept the militia as far from here as possible."

"Yes, sir," she said, switching back to her military role. "I'll have the squad leaders join you."

"Thank you . . . Sara."

"You're welcome, John." She turned and hurried off to find the squad leaders.

As the sun climbed higher into the sky, O'Neill walked around the perimeter of the camp. There were no more than two or three guards posted and awake. One of them sat on the rear of an ATV smoking a cigarette, the orange glow bright even in the increasing sunlight.

"You see anything?" asked O'Neill.

The guard didn't look at him. "Nothin' movin'. Don't 'spect anything to move."

O'Neill didn't respond, but walked on. The party had died a quick death as he had known it would. The people had done too much the day before and had used too much energy.

The bonfire had burned down and the lights of the ATVs had been extinguished but in the growing dawn, he could see the remnants of the party. Bodies scattered everywhere, some of them nude, sleeping in the arms of the partners they'd found for the night. Dawn was going to bring some interesting results. One couple, a man and woman who couldn't stand the sight of each other, were now lying together, arms and legs entwined and not a scrap of cloth between them. Interesting.

Becker appeared, spotted O'Neill, and moved toward him. "Radio from Nast. Wants to know our status now."

"Interesting," said O'Neill. "I don't remember him requesting that information before."

"Nope. I think Starling was giving it to him. Of course, he's not heard from her in over twelve hours."

"You answer the call?"

"Not until I talked to you. What should I tell him?"

"Right now," said O'Neill, "let's just ignore that. Maybe by noon we'll report something. I can't see any advantage in giving him that information."

"Yes, sir."

O'Neill gestured at the sleeping troops and then glanced up at the rising sun. "I think it's time that we hit the road."

"Going to be a lot of sick people today. Too much happened yesterday and they managed to drink a little too much last night."

"Let's start the process," said O'Neill, "but figure it's going to be two hours before we can resume the march. Patience, I think, is the key today."

Becker didn't salute. He turned and moved off, shouting, "Sergeant Pruggs! Sergeant Pruggs!"

The first sergeant appeared suddenly, buckling his pants. O'Neill was close enough to hear Becker issue the orders and Pruggs snap, "Yes, sir. My pleasure."

Pruggs wasted no time. He turned and bellowed. "That's it everyone, reveille. Reveille! On your feet. Let's go." He moved among the soldiers kicking the bottoms of their feet, waiting for a response before moving on.

One woman who wore only a hat glanced up with a surprised look on her face and then leaped to her feet. She ran in a small circle, as if unsure of what to do, her hands moving between her breasts and crotch as she tried to cover herself. Finally she sprinted for an ATV, grabbed a blanket from it and wrapped herself in it.

Laughter erupted from the camp. People were pointing and talking, some shouting at her. One man was laughing so hard he couldn't sit up. He wore a pair of mismatched shoes and nothing more, but he didn't seem to care.

Now the camp was beginning to stir. People were waking, stretching, and more than one was howling in surprise at his or her selection of a partner the night before. Combat did strange things to the human mind.

"First Sergeant," yelled O'Neill. "Let's get the coffee on now."

"Yes, sir." Pruggs whirled on a couple of men and said, "Fire and coffee. Now. Move it."

They took off to search for the mess sergeant and his supply vehicle.

One of the sentries stumbled into the camp dragging his rifle by the barrel, the butt in the dirt. He was bleary-eyed, needed a shave badly, and had hair that stuck out in all directions. It looked as if he'd slept through his tour on guard duty.

O'Neill moved toward him and stepped in front of him. "Where in the hell do you think you're going?"

"Coffee, man."

"You have a job. Back on the perimeter. You'll be relieved later."

"But . . ."

"On the perimeter now or I'll have you shot for desertion."

"You can't . . ."

O'Neill drew his revolver and said, "You want to see?"

"No, sir. Sorry, sir. I misunderstood my orders. I'll return to my post."

O'Neill turned and watched the camp come awake. It wasn't the slow process that he had expected. The men and women got up quickly and then, without much in the way of orders, began to get ready to move out. They packed what needed to be packed, stored it in the ATVs, used the latrines that had been hastily dug far down the slope away from the camp, and then climbed back to find a cup of coffee or a glass of lukewarm juice.

Becker came up to him and said, "I figure another twenty minutes at the most."

With the sun now above the horizon, O'Neill could easily see everything in the camp. Turning, he noticed that some of the deeper valleys were still wrapped in shadows, but they were brightening quickly.

"Then we move out as soon as we can."

"Scouts?"

"Have them report to me. And the lead drivers of the ATVs. I'll give them the route."

"We going to hit the main body today?"

"We're sure as hell going to try. By this time tomorrow, I hope to be on my way home."

"Good," said Becker. "Very good."

"Latest plot on the militia," said Sara, Six One Three, holding a hard-copy map.

John, Six One Two, accepted it and studied it. There was a wide, shallow, valley about forty klicks to the east. Intelligence, according to the map, had projected the militia's route of march through the center of the valley.

"That's the place to intercept them. Right in the middle of the valley where we can see the surrounding territory for miles in all directions."

"I'll get the platoon ready to move out."

John, Six One Two, stopped her. "I'll want to speak to them before we do that. Let them in on the rules that we'll have to follow. All we really want to do is turn them around."

"Yes, sir."

John, Six One Two, looked deep into her eyes. "This is the right thing, isn't it?"

"You're the lieutenant," she said.

"I thought we'd moved beyond that."

She nodded then. "I think that you might be right and therefore we must do this. I just don't like it very much. We're exceeding our authority. We're to watch the militia and report, not intercept them."

"So we made a mistake, got caught, but were able to convince them to return to their base. Everyone's happy."

"I hope so." She stepped away, turned, and walked toward the squad leaders.

In minutes, the platoon was formed in front of him. It was

a loose formation, not the tight, perfect ranks that they fell into on the ship.

John, Six One Two, stood there in front of them, wondering what he should be saying. Finally, to end the silence, he said, "Today we begin our first real assignment. No more training. This is the real world and the real army. Live ammo has been issued and weapons are to be loaded. Today we'll face an armed force of the colonial militia. We are, of course, the superior fighting force. We can defeat any militia operating now. A well-trained, well-equipped regular line unit will always be able to defeat the militias. Training and equipment are the reasons."

He thought about that and then added, "But we're not here to defeat them. We are to turn them from their path and that's all. We are to prevent them from attacking the locals. That must be understood. We are not to fire on them. They are, after all, humans."

Feeling that he'd made his point, he asked, "Are there any questions?"

And like any unit that had spent four years in training together, they responded as a group. "No, sir!"

"Platoon sergeant, take charge of the platoon and have them load the floaters."

Sara, Six One Three, saluted and said, "Yes, sir."

John, Six One Two, watched as the sergeants did their job. The platoon fell out, moved to the four floaters assigned and climbed aboard. When they were loaded, he moved toward the lead craft. He caught Sara, Six One Three, there and ordered her to the trail craft. "We'll be down in about fifteen minutes. Then all we need to do is wait for the militia. By nightfall it should be over."

"Yes, sir. I think that's what's got me worried the most."

"See you in the Valley of Death."

"What?"

"A line from the 'Charge of the Light Brigade.' Into the valley of death rode the six hundred."

"Not part of my training," she said.

John, Six One Two, shrugged. "Then there is something to be said for being the oldest after all."

"Yes, sir," she said. She moved toward the last floater.

John, Six One Two, waited until she had boarded and then entered his. Before he was strapped in, the engine sprang to life and they lifted off. His own words echoed in his head suddenly. Into the valley of death. Suddenly he was frightened.

20

FLAGSHIP OF THE TENTH INTERPLANETARY INFANTRY REGIMENT

IT HAD TAKEN Garvey most of the night to locate Jefferson, though after he'd talked to the doctor with Silvia James half listening, he'd gotten sidetracked. The revelation hadn't seemed quite so important when James had asked if his cabin was occupied. As an ensign, she had roommates, and all were present and accounted for. Garvey had told her that they were close to his and she had led the way.

During the night, Garvey had forgotten about the new platoon and cloning and everything else. He'd watched as James had peeled herself out of her uniform and then climbed onto his bunk, leaning back, watching him.

They'd spent the night thinking of ways of entertaining one another, going from what Garvey considered normal into the realm of the bizarre, not that he cared. His philosophy was to try anything once and if it was fun, to add it to his own closet of tricks.

But then, early in the morning, he'd thought of the platoon and decided that it was time to meet with Jefferson. Let him in on the secret and see if it made any difference in the assignments he was ordering.

Jefferson was in the senior officers' mess with another major and two lieutenant commanders assigned to the ship's company. Jefferson was standing with a glass of juice in his right hand.

"Mister Garvey," he said.

"Been looking for you Colonel. You have a few minutes to spare?"

"Is it important?"

"That remains to be seen. It's something that I think you'd like to know."

"Then join me for some breakfast."

"No, sir," said Garvey. "I think we'd better meet in private."

Jefferson drained the glass and set it on the closest table. To the major, he said, "I'll be back in five minutes or so. See if you can get me some fried eggs and a small steak with hash browns and another glass of juice."

"Certainly. And maybe you'd like a case of cantelopes too," the major said, grinning.

"I'm not on the planet's surface," said Jefferson. "I shall therefore eat well while I can."

"Yes, sir."

Jefferson followed Garvey out into the corridor. There was no one around them. Seeing that they were alone, he said, "Let's have it."

"A question first. What do you know about cloning?"

"It is something that doesn't concern me greatly because it is a scientific matter, not a military one."

"Except you have a platoon that has been cloned."

"Certainly," said Jefferson. "An experimental unit that is temporarily attached to my command. I have seen nothing in their performance to suggest that they are less capable than any of the other units."

Garvey stepped closer and lowered his voice. "The techniques for cloning humans were developed ten years ago."

"So what?" Then his face went white. He shook himself and said, "But they all look to be twenty, twenty-one years old."

"That's what threw me too. But I asked the doctor about that. He told me about techniques for accelerating the growth of certain plants and then animals. What we're seeing is the wave of the future."

"Soldiers, humans designed to be soldiers, grown quickly through childhood and suddenly thrown out into the world."

"I confess," said Garvey. "I was slower on this than you were. I didn't realize it for a couple of hours. It's their bodies that throw you. They can't be kids if they look like that."

Jefferson wasn't interested in the rationalizations. He was

interested in the platoon and the fact that it was manned by kids. He stared at Garvey. "How old are they? Really?"

"The information suggests, based on what I've seen in the last—"

"*How old?*" demanded Jefferson.

"Seven."

"Jesus Christ! Are you sure?"

"Positive."

"Jesus Christ."

The valley was bathed in the morning sun when the first of the floaters touched down. The minute it was on the ground, John, Six One Two, was out of it. He turned to the east and looked at the gentle upsweep of the land. There was no indication that anyone was coming.

The other floaters landed one at a time and the platoon climbed out. They formed a long, ragged line. As they did, the floaters lifted and moved, drifting to the rear, toward a line of trees that marked the banks of the wide, shallow, river.

John, Six One Two, stood with his hands on his hips and slowly surveyed the terrain. There was a ditch to one side that looked as if it might have once been a creek that flowed into the river. One squad could use it as a defensive position.

South of that, closer to the river, was an outcropping of rock. It wasn't very high, two or three feet at its tallest, but it was thirty yards long and would offer another squad a position. One squad would form across the valley floor, along the meandering path that looked like a sometimes-used road, and one squad would be in reserve with the floaters half a klick away.

John, Six One Two, spotted Sara, Six One Three, and said, "First squad to the right, second to the left, third here with me, and fourth join the floaters in the trees."

"Yes, sir. Where should I be?"

"Undercover with the fourth squad," he said. "Where you can observe what happens here when the militia arrive."

"You sure?" she asked.

John, Six One Two, stared at her. "Why are you now questioning everything I order? You never did that during the training exercises."

"Because those were training and the orders were clear. This is not training and you're interpreting your orders to suit yourself."

"You agreed."

"I just want to make sure that you've thought your way through everything."

"I have." He pointed to the rear, where the floaters were concealed in the trees. "That is your post."

"Yes, sir."

"Keep a close watch on us. And the hills around us. The militia may try to make an end run."

"I know my job," she said, her voice harsh. Then it softened. "It'll be all right. We'll get back in the major's good graces. Everything will work out."

"I know. Thanks."

Sara, Six One Three, moved off, taking the fourth squad with her. They trotted along the road for a hundred yards and then diverted to the trees. John, Six One Two, watched the first and second squads filter into their positions, leaving the third standing with him.

"Sergeant, we will form a line across the road. When the militia approaches, everyone will be standing, weapons in hands, rounds chambered and safeties on."

"Yes, sir."

"We do not fire unless they fire first. I don't want a fire fight with them. I just want them to turn. You make sure that your people understand that."

"Yes, sir. How long do you think we'll have to wait?"

John, Six One Two, was going to tell her that he had no idea but before he could speak, he saw a thin column of dust rising in the air beyond the hills. That would be from the ATVs driven by the militia.

"Not long now, I think."

O'Neill liked being in the lead vehicle. That way he didn't have to eat the dust of the others. The column had fragmented slightly as those in the rear had fanned out, trying to avoid as much of the dust as they could. It made for a sloppy-looking formation, but O'Neill didn't care. As long as they all stayed behind him.

They rolled across the long plain, holding the speed down because he didn't know what pitfalls might be concealed in the grass. The scouts had reported nothing, but there was no reason to hurry.

They climbed a low hill and found the scouts sitting just below the crest waiting for them. One man sat on the front of his ATV eating fruit from a can using his knife. O'Neill figured the man had seen too many war movies. That was the only place that soldiers ate using a combat knife.

As they rolled up, O'Neill stood in the back of his ATV, gripped the roll bar, and held up an arm to stop the column. He then jumped over the side and walked toward the man.

"What you got?"

The scout dropped the knife back into the can, wiped his mouth with the back of his hand and said, "Had some activity down there about an hour ago."

"What kind?"

"Looks like the real army has arrived. Floaters and soldiers."

O'Neill climbed to the very top of the slope and raised his binoculars to his eyes. He counted the twelve people he could see. They wore uniforms and held fancy rifles. The uniforms were of the infantry.

"Not too many of them," O'Neill called back, over his shoulder.

"Not now but there were. Couldn't tell how many. Maybe a platoon, maybe more. There's more of them down there than you can see."

O'Neill lowered his binoculars and walked back to the ATV. It was sitting so it would be invisible to the soldiers on the valley floor.

"No reason to worry about them. We're all soldiers. All human. We have common goals."

"They're sitting right across our path," said the scout. "That's something that I don't like."

"We can't afford to go around them and leave them behind us," said O'Neill. "We've got to go down and talk to them. I can't see where that'll be a problem.

The scout lifted the can to his mouth and drank the juice in it. Taking his knife out, he threw the can to the grass. He slipped down from his perch. "Soldiers came down here for a reason. Nast and his people can't be thrilled with the course of events. I'd be careful."

"Thank you but I don't need advice on military strategies from a scout."

"Thought my job was to let you in on my insights as well as the locations of the enemies, whoever they might be."

"Thank you," said O'Neill again. He moved past the ATV and yelled. "Officers' call. Now."

In moments the officers were arranged in front of him. He let them settle down and then said, "There's a contingent of regular infantry in front of us. We're going to have to confront them. I'll take a forward platoon down. Becker, you'll take half the troops in one battalion and follow about a hundred yards behind me, on line. Jones, you'll form the rest of the troops, on line, and climb the hill. You'll wait right here until you get further orders. That understood?"

Jones nodded. "Yes, sir."

"Major Becker?"

"Yes, sir."

"I don't want a fight with these people. We're going down to talk, but we're going to talk from a position of strength. They're not going to push us around just because they're regulars and we're militia."

O'Neill wiped a hand over his face. "One thing I want to stress here. I don't want any shooting. These people are on our side. We'll talk, we'll reason, but there isn't to be any shooting."

"What if they fire first?" asked Becker.

"Then all bets are off. We eliminate the threat as quickly and as efficiently as we can."

"They'll have friends," said Jones. "Lots of friends."

"If they fire on us, I don't care. We'll take them out. Any other questions?"

"No, sir," said Becker.

"Then we move out in five minutes."

Jefferson hadn't wasted any time. He'd left Garvey standing in the corridor as he'd run down it, heading for the communications center. He was going to recall the special platoon until he could get some answers about them. He didn't know much about them, except that they were seven years old. He didn't understand the training they had undergone or what their psychic makeup would be like, but he wasn't going to have an armed force of children in the field. Not until someone explained it to him.

As he reached the mid-lift, he realized that they had acted like adults most of the time. There had been nothing so radical in their behavior that he had suspected that they were anything but twenty-year-old adults. People that age could certainly act immature.

As he entered the mid-lift, he realized that he wasn't that much older than twenty and he, like everyone else, sometimes failed to act his age. The problem, as he understood it, was that he was now afraid that the platoon *would* act its age and that was seven years old.

He hit the buttons on the mid-lift even though it was moving. He wanted it to move faster. He wanted to get the message to Torrence before things could get out of hand.

The doors opened and he bolted from them, running down the corridor. He stopped at the communications center and slammed a hand into the hatch there when it didn't open fast enough. He leaped inside, startling the watch NCO.

"Get me Major Torrence now," Jefferson snapped.

"Major Torrence and her people have . . ."

"I didn't ask for an itinerary. I asked for contact with the major."

"Yes, sir."

The NCO bent to the task, threw the video on the main screen and said, "I've contact with her RTO."

Jefferson pushed himself forward, leaned down and said, "Tell Major Torrence that I want the special platoon recalled at once."

"Yes, sir. I believe that Breaker Six has deployed them."

Jefferson cursed himself for forgetting radio protocol, but then sometimes it got in the way. "Advise Six that the platoon is to be recalled. I want contact with her in zero five."

"Yes, sir." The RTO disappeared from the screen.

The NCO looked at the colonel and asked, "What's the problem, sir."

"None of your damn business." He looked at the chronometer. Where in the hell was Torrence?

A moment later she appeared. "This is Six. Please advise."

"I want the special platoon pulled off the line and formed to be transported back to the shuttle."

"Roger. I've been using them for scouts."

"Major, I did not ask for a discussion. Your mission right now, your only mission, is to get those people out of the field and back here to the ship. Understood?"

"Yes, sir."

"And keep me informed of the progress."

"Yes, sir."

As Torrence's picture faded from the screen, Jefferson looked at the NCO. "I hope to hell that we're not too late."

<u>21</u>

DELTA ROYAL THREE

"HERE THEY COME," yelled one of the platoon members.

John, Six One Two, turned and watched as a single vehicle crested the hill and began the run down toward them. He lifted his binoculars and saw that there were four people riding in it. It seemed that all four were armed.

"Remember," he said. "We do not fire first. There is no reason to fire on them."

A dozen more vehicles appeared and spread out so that they were coming down side by side. A second wave joined the first, sped up, and joined the main line.

"There's a lot of them," said one of the women.

"Doesn't matter," said John, Six One Two. He raised his voice. "First and second squads remain hidden. I'll call for you if I need you."

There was no response from either of the squad leaders.

John, Six One Two, slipped the safety off on his rifle and moved forward so that he was slightly in front of the third squad. They stood behind him, watching the oncoming ATVs.

"Steady," said John, Six One Two. "Follow my lead."

The ATV was closer now. They all could see the features of the people riding in it. John, Six One Two, held up a hand to stop them.

The ATV rolled close and then stopped. One of the men in

the rear stood up. He gripped the roll bar with one hand but held a rifle in the other.

John, Six One Two, walked forward, the barrel of his weapon pointed down at the road in front of the ATV. "Good morning," he said conversationally.

"Morning," said the man standing.

"I'm afraid that you're going to have to turn around." He was aware of all the ATVs behind the man, and now another group had appeared on the hills. There had to be nearly two hundred of them. There might be eight hundred or a thousand people in them. He was suddenly outnumbered twenty or twenty-five to one.

"I'm afraid that we can't do that," said the man. "I have a mission on the far side of the valley. We'll be going forward."

"No," said John, Six One Two. "My orders are quite clear on this point."

"And I'm afraid that we're going forward."

"I have my orders . . ."

"Which mean nothing here. We are a duly constituted militia under orders of the colonial government and Commissioner Nast. Now, clear the path or we will roll over you."

"Sir, I have my orders. You are not to pass this point."

The man laughed, throwing his head back. He laughed long and loud, sounding as if he'd heard the funniest joke in the world. The funniest joke ever told.

Finally getting himself under control, he asked, "The twelve of you?"

"There are more of us," said John, Six One Two.

Without waiting for orders, the first squad stood. They leveled their weapons.

"Even that many won't cause us too much trouble," said the man. "We'll roll over you."

"If you mean to have war," said John, Six One Two, his voice rising. "Then start it here and now. But know one thing. There is a fleet in space holding a trained combat regiment. They back us up."

"Won't do you any good if you're dead," said the man.

"If we die, then you will too. You'll be the first to die," said John, Six One Two.

"That, my friend, sounds like a threat."

"Shit, Colonel. Shoot the little bastard and let's be done with it," yelled one of the men. "I've had enough of this bullshit. Fucking outsiders sticking their noses in where they don't belong."

"Hold it down," said the man.

And then a single shot rang out. It hit nothing, but everyone dove for cover. The men in the ATVs leaped over the side. The squad scattered, right and left.

For a moment it looked as if the one shot would be ignored. No one was hit, no one was hurt. No damage had been done. John, Six Two One, leaning with his back against a rock yelled, "Who fired?"

The rippling came from the enemy line. A ragged volley that slammed into the rocks. Bullets whined off, tumbling upward and away.

"Fire," yelled someone. "FIRE!"

John, Six One Two, spun, came up on his knees and saw one line of the ATVs racing down on them. He flipped the selector switch to full auto and opened fire. There was a quick hammering as the shells flashed in the morning sun. The empty casings bounced crazily, the sun sparkling.

When his weapon was empty, he dropped down. Glancing to the right he saw two bodies laying on the grass. There was blood splattered on one and pooling under the other. A brother and sister had been hit. For a moment he didn't think about it. He could only hear the sounds of the firing and the roaring of the ATV engines as they came at them.

"Kill them," yelled John, Six One Two. "Kill them all."

Now all those with him were firing. The sounds of the rifles mixed. It was a single, drawn out detonation. There was screaming. From the wounded. From the angry. From a hundred throats on both sides.

John, Six One Two, reloaded and popped up. An ATV was aimed at him, the men and women in it firing as the vehicle bounced along. He aimed at the windshield and saw it star and then shatter under the impact of his rounds. The driver's face exploded in blood. The ATV turned sharply, up on three wheels. The people jumped from it as it rolled over. Two were cut down by the intense fire. Another two took several running steps and were killed.

"Don't let them close," yelled, John, Six One Two. "Don't let them close."

Two other vehicles overturned and a third burst into flames. There was a muffled explosion and then a louder one. Flaming debris rained down.

And then, just as quickly as it had started, it was over. The ATVs that could retreated toward the hill. John, Six One Two, stood and fired at them, pumping rounds into them. A man stood and fell out. Another vehicle swerved and crashed. Three of the passengers leaped up to run.

"Hold your fire," ordered John, Six One Two. "Hold your fire."

"We've got wounded," yelled a female voice. "We need help."

"We've got dead," said another. "Two dead."

John, Six One Two, turned and walked to the bodies. He crouched down and looked at them. Both seemed to be smaller now. Both smelled of hot copper. Neither moved nor breathed. They were dead.

He felt tears in his eyes as he looked up at his brothers and sisters surrounding him. "Why?" he asked. "Who fired? Who would start this?"

"One of them," said a brother. "They started it because they're stupid jerks."

"We need a medic," yelled a voice.

"Short-com," said John, Six One Two. "Get the floaters here and bring up the reserve. Floaters for the wounded."

"Yes, sir."

John, Six One Two, stood and turned, looking back at the enemy. The real enemy and for the first time in his short life he felt true hatred.

O'Neill stood on the hilltop and looked at the burning wreckage of half a dozen ATVs. Fifty bodies were scattered among the debris. Fifty of his friends. He didn't like the losses. It was the first time that one of his assaults had been repelled.

Becker, along with Jones, Pruggs and Helen Byrd came up behind him. As they did, the floaters appeared, coming from the distant tree line.

"They're getting reinforcements."

"Not many," said O'Neill. "Might double their strength. Might not."

"We'd better hit them fast," said Becker. "If we don't,

we're going to have trouble getting our people to attack. Not with the losses we've already taken."

There was a wailing scream behind them that was cut off suddenly. Byrd said, "We've got twenty wounded, four of them bad. They're going to die if we don't get them help."

O'Neill pointed at the enemy below him. "Those floaters could get us to the town in a matter of minutes. Not the hours the ATVs would take. Save some of our wounded."

"We'll have to move quickly," said Becker again.

"I heard that." O'Neill wiped the sweat from his face. "I want three companies. Two to hit the flanks and one to go straight at them. Divide their firepower by worrying about all of us. One company will penetrate their perimeter and, once that happens, their defense will collapse."

"When?"

O'Neill looked at the assembled officers. Byrd was standing with tears in her eyes. She knew what this meant. More people were going to die and she didn't want to hear about it.

O'Neill checked the time. "I think we'd better do it now. As soon as we can get the troops divided into the attack companies."

"Yes, sir."

O'Neill had faced these people more than once in the last few days in a similar situation. They were about to attack the enemy. And still there didn't seem to be anything to say to them. Finally, he said, "Report ready status as soon as possible."

Becker answered for all of them. "Yes, sir."

John, Six One Two, watched the floaters come up out of the woods, hover there for a moment and then turn toward him. He waved a hand, knowing that it wouldn't speed them. "Come on," he yelled.

The first of the floaters dipped its nose and then ran along the ground, no more than three or four feet above it. The wash from the engine stirred the dust creating the illusion of a vapor trail.

"Get the wounded ready to load," said John, Six One Two. Then he saw Shelia, Seven Four Eight, sitting on the ground, a rag around her thigh. Blood stained it. Her face was waxy, looking almost artificial.

She saw him watching her and tried to grin. "I'll be okay," she said. "Molly, Eight One Nine, should take over for me."

"She'll do fine. You sure you're okay?"

"Yes, I'll be fine. Little hole in my leg. Give me some character. Now you'll be able to tell me from all our sisters."

"I could always tell you apart."

"Sure."

The floater approached and settled to the ground. Sara, Six One Three, leaped from it. She looked at the battlefield, the smoking wrecks of the ATVs, the dead and wounded, and then rushed to John, Six One Two.

His face was dirty, a smear of mud along his chin. Sweat stained his uniform. As Sara, Six One Three, approached, he said, "They'll come back. Get the platoon organized."

"Yes, sir."

He turned back and watched as the badly wounded were loaded. One of the men was missing an arm. Another's chest was covered with blood and his breathing was labored, a wheezing gasp that whistled in his throat. Shelia, Seven Four Eight, was half carried on by two others. She limped badly, refusing to put a strain on her wounded leg.

"Could have been worse," said Sara, Six One Three.

John, Six One Two, looked at the bodies of his brothers and sisters being loaded into the floater. He could almost feel the pain of their deaths. Could almost understand what they felt. His body ached and he was light-headed. It was difficult to concentrate. Sara, Six One Three, didn't seem to have that problem. Maybe it was because she had been separated from them during the short fight.

"They're on the move," yelled a sister. She pointed up at the enemy as the ATVs began to roll north and south.

John, Six One Two, moved to the rocks and leaned across the top of one. It was hot from the sun, but he didn't notice that. He raised his binoculars. The enemy was preparing for an attack, that was obvious, but it didn't seem he would be coming very soon.

Turning, John, Six One Two, said, "Sara, spread the final squad behind us so that the enemy can't attack from the rear. Be prepared to fill in if the defense begins to collapse."

"Yes, sir. Should we radio for assistance?"

John, Six One Two, considered the question and then

rejected it. He had to stop the enemy on his own. To do less would be to fail. He was already in trouble with Major Torrence, and if he couldn't stop the rabble that faced him, he would be stripped of his command. He knew that.

"No. We can handle them."

"At what price?" she asked quietly, her voice barely above a whisper.

The appearance of a floater heading toward them at top speed surprised Torrence. One of the sentries called out that it was coming just as the tracking system in the commo pod picked it up. The RTO yelled, "They've got wounded."

"What the hell?" yelled Torrence. She whirled and ordered, "Medics."

"Coming up now."

The floater screamed over the tops of the trees. The nose popped up suddenly as if it was about to climb into orbit, but the roar of the engine decreased rapidly and the cloud of dust whirling around it dissipated as it settled to the ground. As it touched down, the medics rushed toward it.

Torrence saw a woman with a thick bandage around her thigh lifted from the floater and then set on the ground. She didn't seem to be in any immediate danger. Torrence moved toward her. "What the hell is going on?"

"The militia attacked us."

"What do you mean attacked?" demanded Torrence. "You were supposed to observe, not fight."

"They attacked us. We had to defend ourselves."

A medic moved in, crouched over the woman, and began to work at the bandage. The wounded woman gritted her teeth and sucked air.

"Sorry." The medic continued to work, finally freeing the bandage. There was a neat hole in the leg, some blood, but no other damage. "You're lucky. Missed the artery and the bone. Couple of days and you'll be fine."

"Can I get back to the platoon?"

"Not today."

"What happened?" demanded Torrence again.

"We blocked the road to stop the militia and turn them back. They fired on us and we shot back."

"Where's the rest of the platoon?"

"Still there," said the woman.

To the medic, Torrence said, "What's your agenda here?"

"Get the wounded back to the fleet where they can get the treatment they need."

"Fine." Torrence spun and ran toward the commo pod. As she approached, she shouted, "Get me a link with the colonel and get it now."

"Yes, ma'am."

As soon as the link was established, Torrence said, "We've got a problem. That special platoon has been attacked."

"What?"

"They apparently tried to turn the militia and it erupted into a fire fight. We've got dead and wounded. Some are coming up to the fleet now."

"Where's the platoon?"

"Still in the field."

"Get them out now!" ordered Jefferson. "I don't care what you do, but get them out of there now!"

22

DELTA ROYAL THREE

"I DON'T LIKE, this," said Sara, Six One Three. "They're going to hit us on three sides at once."

"I know that," said John, Six One Two. "We've got to figure a way to outgun them."

"Can't be done. Too many of them and too few of us," she said. "Though an automatic weapon can make up a lot of the difference."

"And if our people aim at them. Really aim and not just throw out rounds, that could be the difference in the fight."

"Yes, sir."

John, Six One Two, wiped a hand over his sweat-streaked face. He'd learned that men in war fired their weapons sometimes just to be firing them. They didn't aim, and when armies started equipping soldiers with automatic weapons, the problem became worse. They threw out clouds of bullets, firing as fast as they could, but without aiming. The theory was that with enough lead in the air, the enemy would get hit.

But, when outnumbered by more than twenty to one, the soldiers had to aim. Had to make the shots count, because they couldn't afford a battle of attrition. They'd lose that in a matter of minutes.

"Talk to the squad leaders. Tell them to make sure that every shot counts. It's our only hope."

"Yes, sir." Sara, Six One Three, turned and began moving among the troops, spreading the word.

John, Six One Two, turned and saw that the ATVs were now facing down the slopes, pointed at him and his tiny command. They sat there for a moment, on the hillside, looking like Indians about to wipe out the wagon train. Then, suddenly, they began to rush forward. A cloud of dust erupted from behind the wheels, marking the line of departure.

"Here they come again," yelled a male voice.

John, Six One Two, stood where he was and ordered. "Hold your fire. Hold your fire."

It was almost impossible to stand there while the enemy roared down on him. But he didn't want the impact of the initial volley dissipated. If the enemy was closer, more shots would hit their targets. If enough of the enemy was killed, then they might just turn to flee. If.

"Wait for it," he yelled. "Wait for it." He wanted to shoot. To stop them. They were still half a klick away but closing fast. "Just a moment." Then suddenly, he knew it was time. "NOW!"

It was like a drawn-out explosion as the platoon opened fire, all of them on full auto. ATVs swerved and one of them flipped, spilling the occupants from it. Another burst into flames, black smoke boiling up into the sky.

Firing came from the enemy, not just those in front, but those rolling in from the sides. Bullets snapped through the air, slammed into the rocks or the ground or ricochetted off. Little puffs of dust erupted around them.

The man crouched next to John, Six One Two, suddenly stood up, blood pouring from a wound in his side. He looked at it, tried to put a hand on it and then toppled to the ground.

There were screams now. The ATVs were closer. John, Six One Two, could see the faces of the people in them. He could see them firing at him. Puffs of smoke from the muzzles of their weapons. He ducked, heard rounds smash into the rocks, and then popped up again to fire. He watched dust fly from the shirts of the men he hit in the front of an ATV. The driver slumped but the vehicle raced forward. Someone in the back bailed out, took a running step and then fell, rolling over and over.

The vehicles were closer now but they began to swerve,

starting to circle the platoon. They fired continuously, the rounds dancing in the dirt around their position. Two ATVs hit, bounced off and then both began to burn. People leaped from them and were shot down immediately.

John, Six One Two, dropped down, his head far below the top of the rocks so that he could reload. He spotted Sara, Six One Three, standing up, aiming carefully, like she was on the firing line, practicing against cardboard targets. Rounds were flashing around her but she took no notice.

O'Neill knew that it was going to be costly. The first skirmish had proven that. They were facing an armed force who knew what they were doing. They held the only defensible position on the valley floor and there were about fifty of them armed with automatic weapons. As long as their ammo held up, they were going to kill people.

He rode in one of the lead ATVs, but was hunched down in the seat so that he could barely see over the dashboard. He kept his eyes on the enemy, waiting for them to begin firing, wondering why they didn't.

And then the enemy position erupted in flame and fire. The windshield shattered and one of the men in the back was hit. He slumped, his blood splashing over the rear of the seat. The odor of hot copper filled the air.

"Kill them," yelled O'Neill. "Wipe them out." He leaned around the windshield and aimed, but the bouncing vehicle made a lousy firing platform. He couldn't steady his aim. He pulled the trigger anyway, just to be firing. Maybe it would make the enemy dive for cover.

They raced forward, closing on the enemy. He could see them popping up, firing, and dropping back. Their firing was accurate. One of the ATVs exploded. Another tipped over. Men fell as they were hit.

As they got close to the enemy, the firing increased. More people died as more ATVs were destroyed. The leaders then swerved to the right, running to the north. The men and women leaned out, firing into the enemy soldiers.

O'Neill wanted to run straight on to them, but couldn't. The firing was too intense. Too many people were getting hit. He let his driver swerve.

He twisted around, looking down at the dead man in the

back of his ATV. There was a single hole in the man's bloodless face. Crimson stained everything. Beyond the dead man, were the other ATVs, turning to follow. Men and women firing out of them.

The attack was beginning to falter and O'Neill didn't know what to do about it. Turning back in toward the enemy would do no good. His troops wanted to maintain a little distance as they whittled down the numbers of the enemy.

"More on the south," yelled one of his sisters. "Coming on fast."

"Stop them," ordered John, Six One Two.

He saw Sara, Six One Three, finally leap for cover. She rolled to her back and lifted her face, grinning at him. He nodded at her and wanted to tell her that she was extremely brave. And extremely stupid.

With his weapon reloaded, he popped up, aimed at one of the circling ATVs and fired. A short burst. The rounds stuck the side of the vehicle and punched through. One of the riders lost the grip on her rifle and dropped it.

Those attacking from the south were getting closer. They drove straight on, even in the face of the heavy fire. John, Six One Two, turned and aimed at them, emptying his magazine.

A wounded sister dropped near him. She climbed unsteadily to her hands and knees and looked at him with a blood-soaked face. She tried to speak, failed, grinned, and then collapsed.

John, Six One Two, crouched near her as if protecting her. He fired at the enemy. One man died, but the ATVs kept coming. These weren't going to turn.

"On the north."

John, Six One Two, spun and saw that the first assault group had joined the second in a huge mass and all were bearing down on his position. He slowly stood up so that he could see better, knowing that he'd made a mistake. The enemy was too strong for them. They were going to be overrun in a matter of minutes.

"Radio," he yelled. "I want the radio."

One of the brothers, Jack, Two Three Seven, stood and ran toward him. As John, Six One Two, grabbed the hand set, Jack, Two Three Seven, was hit in the back. He was lifted from his feet and thrown to the ground. He lost his grip on his rifle, letting it spin away from him. He was dead as he hit the dirt.

"Oh, God," wailed John, Six One Two. "What have I done?" He grabbed the handset but there was no carrier wave. The radio was as dead as the man who had carried it into battle.

A sister standing close to the rocks was hit. She spun and fell, blood on her chest. She looked up, met John, Six One Two's, eyes for a moment. Then her's filmed over as she died.

"Pull back," he yelled. "Pull back." He wanted to consolidate his position. Reduce the size of the perimeter so that everyone could support everyone else. It was the last tactic he had. Form what the British had called the square. Everyone standing with someone to his or her back. Everyone defending everyone else. It was an act of desperation.

O'Neill watched as more of the enemy platoon fell. The firing from them was decreasing as the soldiers died. Now the attack from the south had bled off some of their strength. Joining with Becker, who was coming from the north, they would overwhelm the enemy. In minutes the battle would be over. All of them would be dead.

His ATVs, without an order from him, turned to join Becker as they began their run toward the enemy. Firing erupted from them. Poorly aimed shots, but that didn't matter. It drew their attention, forcing them to meet the new threat.

O'Neill stood up, a hand on the bullet-scarred windshield of his ATV. He waved a hand and pointed. Bullets snapped through the air close to him but he ignored them. It was time to end the battle. End it quickly.

More of the enemy fell. They dropped singly or in twos and threes. Their firing slowly tapered as the soldiers were wounded and killed. Fewer men and women to fire back at the attackers.

Over the wind of the rushing ATV and the firing of his own troops, he screamed, "Take them all now. Kill them all now." He fired once, and then dropped his rifle to the ground. He pulled his pistol but didn't fire it. He would use it to kill the wounded when they had overrun the enemy position.

Around him the ATVs spread out into a long, curving line. Clouds of dust rose behind them as their wheels tore up the loose soil and the dried grass. O'Neill ignored all that, keeping his attention on the platoon dying in front of him.

He hadn't thought that they would be so tenacious. He had thought that throwing out a wall of lead would turn them and chase them from the field. He hadn't expected the repeated assaults that were wearing down his soldiers, killing more of them.

"Here they come again," yelled someone.

"Open fire," ordered, John, Six One Two. "Everybody. Open fire."

The ATVs stopped five hundred yards away, and half the militia leaped from them, fanning out in a long skirmish line. Some of them threw themselves to the ground and began to fire at the platoon.

Then, one man stood up in front of an ATV and waved a hand. As one, the vehicles leaped forward, rushing down toward the platoon.

Around him the platoon increased the rate of fire. The hammering of the weapons filled the air, obliterating all other sounds except for the whine of the engines at high speed.

John, Six One Two, stood his ground, his rifle to his shoulder. He aimed low remembering a hundred tapes that told him the tendency in battle was to shoot high. He held the trigger down, burned through the magazine and felt the bolt lock back. He slipped to one knee, ripped the empty magazine from the weapon, tossed it aside, and reloaded. He looked up to see that the ATVs were closer. Much closer.

He aimed at the sun-winking windshield of one and fired. The windshield exploded inward and the ATV swerved to the right, hit the vehicle next to it and both of them overturned. Militia spilled out. They used the wrecked ATVs for cover, firing at the platoon.

Rounds began to hit the rocks near him. Chipped stone clipped him, stinging his face. He felt a rivulet of blood dribble, but ignored it. He fired at the enemy soldiers. His rounds slammed into the ATVs.

Then, without warning, pain flaired in his back. Sudden, stunning pain. The world turned red and then white. He felt something hit his face, not realizing that he had fallen forward. He could hear the shooting all around him, could hear shouting, and the roaring of engines, but he didn't know what was happening. Something had changed and he had no idea what it was.

For ten seconds it looked as if the platoon would be destroyed by the colonial militia, but then Torrence and the floaters carrying the first company of her provisional battalion flashed over the crest of the hill. In an instant she could see what was happening. The ATVs roaring down on the beleaguered defense. The platoon was badly outnumbered.

"Spread out," she ordered.

The floaters fanned out so that they were moving on line, heading down into the battle. Using the short com, she said, "Platoon leaders, you'll have charge of your platoons as we hit the ground. First platoon, your assignment is to punch through to the people on the ground and strengthen the perimeter. Second platoon and third platoons, you'll hit the group on the north. Fourth platoon, you take them on the south. Report in platoon order."

"One, roger."

"Two, roger."

"Three, roger."

"Four, roger."

To the floater pilot, she said, "You land us ten yards from the platoon, in the center of the formation."

"Roger that."

She took a moment to check her weapon, knowing full well it was loaded and the safety was on. She snapped it off as she felt the floater's nose lift, signalling the landing.

As it touched down, she ran from it, heading straight to the middle of the platoon's perimeter. Her company was moving too, running to take up their firing positions. They were shooting as they moved.

The ATV attack faltered as the fresh troops joined the battle. Each of the soldiers fired, the two hundred automatic weapons hammering as they spread out.

O'Neill watched in horror as the floaters appeared over the hills and then dived for the battlefield. He knew that they could take the unit in front of him but the cost was growing rapidly. Too many of his soldiers were dying. Too many of the vehicles had been wrecked. Now there were more soldiers coming to join that trapped unit. More than enough to overwhelm his militia. The tide had suddenly turned.

O'Neill dropped down into the seat and slapped the shoulder of the driver. "Get us out of here."

"Sir?"

"Let's get out of here."

The driver spun the wheel, turning sharply. A rooster's tail of dust flew, concealing them for a moment. They then rocketed forward, now climbing the gentle slope that would lead to safety.

O'Neill twisted in the seat. He ignored the bloody corpse behind him. He lifted his rifle and fired back at the enemy soldiers. He worked the bolt, ejecting a shell, and fired again.

Around him he was aware of other ATVs turning to flee. No order for a retreat had to be issued. They all could see that he was getting out. They would follow him in that too.

Over the noise, the driver shouted, "I don't like running away."

"He who runs away lives to fight another day," screamed O'Neill. "Too many soldiers now. Only thing we can do is get out."

"Shit!"

O'Neill emptied his rifle and then worked to reload it, his head down. Something punched into the seat behind him, slamming him forward. Pain flared in his back, low, near his spine. It was as if his pants had suddenly caught fire. He leaped up, standing for a moment. A second round hit him in the head, shoving him forward. He grabbed at the edge of the windshield, missed, and fell from the vehicle. He rolled over twice and landed facing up into the bright blue sky. It seemed that the sun was going out, fading away, as everything turned black. And then he was aware of nothing else.

The ATVs were raked with a devastating fire. They swerved, overturned, exploded, and burst into flames. The passengers leaped clear of them, many of them cut down before they could flee. Others threw down their weapons and tried to surrender. Firing increased, sounding like a hundred chain saws attacking a virgin forest. Tracers flashed and rounds snapped through the morning air.

And then the firing tapered. A few of the ATVs gained the high ground a mile or more from the battlefield. They didn't stop there, but kept going, disappearing over the ridge lines.

From the time that Torrence and her company landed, to the destruction of the enemy assault, ninety-seven seconds had passed.

She lowered her weapon as the firing became sporadic and then died out completely. Some of her people began to filter out from the perimeter, moving to disarm those who had surrendered. To round them up.

Torrence looked at the destruction around her. She saw the dozens of burning vehicles. The bodies scattered everywhere, becoming more numerous the closer she looked to the perimeter. Maybe two hundred dead. Maybe more.

And around her were the remnants of the platoon. She spotted Sara, Six One Three, standing alone, her rifle in one hand. Torrence knew it was Sara, Six One Three, because of the rank insignia she wore.

She walked over to her and said, "Where is the lieutenant?"

Sara, Six One Three, looked up at Torrence. Tears stained her face. She looked sick. Pale. Looked as if she was about to pass out.

"You hit?" asked Torrence.

Sara, Six One Three, shook her head. "No." She was silent for a minute and then said, "So many of them are dead. So many of my brothers and sisters are dead." She turned and looked up at Torrence, staring right into her eyes. "What's going to happen to us now? What's going to happen?"

"Where's the lieutenant?"

Sara, Six One Three, shrugged as if she didn't know, and then pointed. "There."

Torrence saw the body lying near the rocks. Blood stained the back of the shirt. It was a huge, wet, stain and the body looked shrunken, as if most of the blood had been drained.

"Lieutenant's dead," said Sara, Six One Three. "Just as we began to know him. Just as we started to become a family. A real family."

One of Torrence's officers appeared, but he didn't salute. "Got the area secured. Probably have two hundred, two hundred and fifty prisoners."

"Keep them separated from the rest of our people. You have security out?"

"Yes, ma'am. There won't be a counterattack now."

"Have Martuesi bring the other company up. I'll want her to run down those who escaped. Turn them over to the colonial government."

"Colonials won't do anything about this."

Torrence looked at him for a moment and said, "Doesn't matter. You have your orders."

"Yes, ma'am."

"Get the medics working and send one over here."

"Yes, ma'am." The young officer turned and ran off.

Torrence now looked back at Sara, Six One Three. She stood still, not moving, looking as if she was about catatonic. Torrence reached out and touched her arm. "I know how you feel."

"How can you know?" flared Sara, Six One Three. "How can anybody know? These people weren't just fellow soldiers. They were my brothers and sisters. It's like a piece of me died. A great piece. You can't know." She pointed at John, Six One Two, laying face down by the rocks. "How can you know what they did to him? What you did."

"Me?"

"He was afraid that you disapproved of that episode in the NCO quarters that he wanted to prove his worth to you. To you and the colonel."

Torrence shook her head. "What are you talking about?"

"Last night . . . was it only last night? When you caught us playing poker . . ."

"No one cared about that," said Torrence.

"Oh, God, then this was all for nothing." She fell to her knees, bent at the waist and began to cry uncontrollably. "It was all for nothing."

23

FLAGSHIP OF THE TENTH INTERPLANETARY
INFANTRY REGIMENT

IT WAS ONE hell of a story, thought Garvey. The best that he'd found since he'd come aboard the ship to report on the activities of one of the few living holders of the Galactic Silver Star. A hell of a story that would make a hell of an impact.

He looked at his notes, scribbled on bits of paper, a napkin, and in a small notebook. He refused to use the computer to organize his notes because he couldn't spread them out enough. He liked having a hundred pieces of paper. It was easier that way.

He came across the one that said simply, "Seven years old." He shook his head. Seven. Little kids in adult bodies. That explained so much. The temper tantrums that he, along with others, had written off to immaturity. If only they had understood that.

The scientific brains had accelerated the growth of the bodies and forgotten about the minds. Taught them everything they needed to know about the military but forgot the social graces. Brought them along slowly when dealing with the military arts and neglected to say a thing about the sexual differences between boys and girls.

The poor little bastards.

But it was still a hell of a story.

Seven years old and they had never been outside the military environment. They had been bred from the genes of an old soldier, but no one knew who. Just a good soldier and, given what happened, Garvey wondered if someone hadn't found a way of duplicating the genes of George Armstrong Custer. He'd tried to stop a numerically superior force. The difference was that he didn't have a provisional battalion that could ride to his rescue. He was on his own when he rode down on the Little Bighorn.

Thirty-two of them had been killed, including the one trained as the lieutenant, John, Six One Two. Dead at seven, fighting in a battle that none of them understood.

Thirty-two of them.

Thirty-two of them who had never had the chance to live. Who didn't know anything other than the army. Who didn't understand the feelings in their own bodies.

Garvey remembered how he had been at nineteen and twenty. The feelings that he was inadequate, the hormones that raged, coloring his thinking, and he'd had nineteen or twenty years of experience to fall back on. These kids had nothing at all. They were just suddenly nineteen or twenty years old physically but only seven mentally.

Hypno tanks, behavior modification, and military training is not the same as living for nineteen years and feeling the changes come on slowly. An awakening of sexual urges, a socialization process that is developed over the years, is necessary to understand what is happening. It's not adequate either, but it's a hell of a lot better than just waking up one morning and finding out you're nineteen and boys and girls are different.

There was a quiet bong at the hatch. Garvey touched a key on the computer and the screen showed that Jefferson and Torrence were standing outside his hatch. He opened it but didn't get out of his chair.

Jefferson came in and looked around. "Seems you have good accommodations. Almost as good as mine."

"Almost," he said suspiciously. "You've never come down here before. I've always got to go in search of you."

"Well," said Torrence, "this time we came to see you."

"So, what do you want?"

Jefferson glanced at Torrence as if seeking support. Then, as he sat on the edge of the cot, he said, "We heard that you've been asking questions about the special platoon."

"Some."

"We think that it's a story that doesn't need to be told now," said Jefferson.

"Protecting the jerks that engineered this nightmare?"

Torrence shook her head. "We hadn't even thought of them. We were more concerned with the platoon's survivors. What this means to them. Sara, the platoon sergeant, is practically useless now. She's like . . . what, lost. Unable to function, as if half her brain is suddenly missing."

"And the others," said Jefferson, "aren't much better. They've all got psychological problems. It's as if most of the people in their world had suddenly disappeared. As if they had been abandoned."

"But this is a story that has to get out," said Garvey. "If they've done it once, they'll do it again."

"We're reporting a complete failure, which, of course, it was," said Jefferson. "They didn't understand some of the finer points of living in a social environment. Their lieutenant was separated from them so that he never had the chance to interact with people. The NCOs had it a little better because they interacted with each other. And the platoon itself only interacted with other members of the platoon."

"I know all that," said Garvey.

Torrence brushed a hand through her hair. "They're all basket cases now. Our doctors think, with the right counseling they might recover . . ."

"Except they're only seven years old," said Garvey.

"Kids," said Jefferson. "Little kids. God, I can't believe they'd try something like that."

"That's why I have to write the story," said Garvey. "So that they won't be able to do it again."

"He's got a point," said Torrence.

"Our concern," said Jefferson, "are the survivors. We don't want them to end up as freaks in a sideshow. See the adult seven year old. He walks, he talks, he doesn't have a clue about society."

"I have a question," said Garvey. "What about the colonial service people?"

Now Jefferson smiled. "That was a sideshow and one worth

the price of admission. Nast tried to blame everything on the head of the militia, guy named O'Neill who managed to get himself killed in the battle. Becker, his deputy, survived and tried to do in Nast for calling us in. The head of this whole region reviewed the data, found that a slaughter of the locals had been committed by O'Neill with the tacit approval of Nast. Nast was removed, emissaries were sent to negotiate with the locals. The only viable solution was for us to abandon the planet. Wasn't ours to settle, the locals have no concept of land ownership, and each local speaks only for himself or herself, and not even for those living in the same village."

"Very idealistic," said Garvey, "but you know what's going to happen."

"Sure," said Jefferson. "Someone is going to remember this lush little planet and we'll return to start over, but for the moment the locals are safe from us."

Garvey turned and looked at his notes. It was a hell of a story. He pushed all the slips of paper into a pile. He stared at it for a moment and said, "I'll hold off on the story. For a while, anyway."

"At least until we can do something for the platoon," said Jefferson.

"But I'm going to write it," cautioned Garvey. "It's a story that must be told."

Jefferson stood. "I couldn't agree more. But not right now."

With Torrence, he moved to the hatch. Garvey watched them exit, then looked at his notes. A great story, but one that would have to wait.

Now he stood and wondered what Silvia James was doing, since he no longer had a story to write. Moments after Jefferson and Torrence left, Garvey exited. It was the only thing he could do.